VERA KELLY IS NOT A MYSTERY

VERA KELLY IS NOT A MYSTERY

ROSALIE KNECHT

THORNDIKE PRESS
A part of Gale, a Cengage Company

**LIBRARY OF CONGRESS CIP DATA ON FILE.
CATALOGUING IN PUBLICATION FOR THIS BOOK
IS AVAILABLE FROM THE LIBRARY OF CONGRESS.**

ISBN-13: 978-1-4328-8702-5 (hardcover alk. paper)

Published in 2021 by arrangement with Tin House

Printed in Mexico
Print Number: 01   Print Year: 2021

For Ambrose

For Ambrose

■ ■ ■ ■

I
AUGUST 1967

BROOKLYN, NY

■ ■ ■ ■

CHAPTER 1

The morning after Jane left me, I woke in a Russian diner that overlooked the boardwalk at Brighton Beach, sitting upright in the corner of a booth. I had always been grateful for an all-night restaurant. A waitress with red cheeks was refilling the cup of coffee in front of me and rotating the plate with its scraps of corned beef, clearing her throat politely. I sat up and thanked her. Through the fogged glass I could see the gray ocean, pale and soft, meeting a paler sky. Down the beach, the Wonder Wheel at Coney Island was coming out of the predawn dark. I put my hand over the mug and the waitress moved away.

By my watch, it was 6:40 in the morning, which meant that it was almost twenty-four hours now since things had begun to go wrong. Jane had said, "I'm tired of waiting for you to want me here." She was standing in the hallway between my bedroom and the second-floor bathroom, holding the powder-pink bag with her makeup and toothbrush in it, wearing my dressing gown. "I don't have to move in. But you hardly talk to me."

"I talk to you."

"About what? About nothing. I turn around and you've left the room."

"I talk to you."

"You say clever things, and when I try to answer you seriously, you make clever jokes."

"You can move in, then," I said, becoming desperate. "You can move in. I've been stupid."

"You know I can't. You would make me miserable." She waved her hand toward the hall, the stairs. "You practically faint when I leave my shoes on the rug." She brushed past me to my room. I leaned in the doorway and watched her getting dressed. My eyes were stinging, my nose was stinging. I sneezed. "I have a class to teach," she said. "I'll get the rest of my things later."

"Don't go," I said. I said it into my cupped hand.

She put her hand on my shoulder. "You're a nice girl, Vera," she said. "But you're impossible."

Jane was noisy and hot, with a bright face;

10

after she left, the house felt like a meat locker, despite the August weather. I went for a long, blurry walk. When I got home, I stood in the kitchen for fifteen minutes, looking at the wall clock, and then had a whiskey and sat in the garden. The roses were blooming for the second time that year. They were yellow washed with pink, like sherbet melting in a bowl of punch. The starling who lived under the eaves of the shed came out to scream at me. He thought the yard was his. It was ten o'clock in the morning. It was time to go to work.

I was one of the film editors for the news broadcast at the WKNY station near the Battery. I started leaking tears on the Q train over the river, because the view was too big and I could see the trees on Governors Island, fizzing and dark in the sun. The summer would be over soon.

I made it to my break before I called her. She had a telephone in her office at Brooklyn College, and she would have just finished her afternoon Romantic poetry class. It rang twice and she picked up.

"Jane?" I said. "I think this is a mistake. I'll make it up to you."

"Vera, it's too late. All right? I'm sorry."

"What do you mean?" I was alone in the editing room, and I was keeping my voice low. George Kepler must have been listening from the switchboard, or patched in from another office. Later, I wondered if he had been listening to my calls for months, ever since he had cornered me at the bar where the editors and runners went after the evening broadcast and I had pushed him off, laughing.

"What do you mean, it's too late?" I said. "Is there someone else?"

She said nothing.

"Christ, Jane. Is there? There is?"

"I didn't plan it this way."

I hung up and tried not to fall apart. My eyes were rattling in my head. I went to the stairwell and smoked a cigarette, and then another. I returned to the editing room. My supervisor, Mr. Anderson, was there, standing with George Kepler, who looked very pleased.

"Vera, I need to speak with you," Mr. Anderson said, and turned to indicate his office with a sweep of his hand, as if we were going to the theater together.

"What for?" I said. George Kepler turned and walked away. The hairs on the back of my neck were standing up.

"Privately," he said.

He shut the door behind us and pointed to a chair. His windows looked out on a post

office lot, with a huge doorway to an under-
ground garage where fleets of mail trucks
came and went in the gloom. Sunlight never
touched the street in this part of town.

"There's a character clause in your employment contract," he said. He looked at
me as if I should grasp his meaning, and
then I did. A mask descended. I tried to
keep my voice calm.

"Can you make yourself clear?" I said. "I
have a lot of work to do."

"No, you don't," he said. "You're in viola-
tion of your employment contract. We can't
keep people on staff who live that way." He
pushed back from his desk and began
searching in his coat pocket for his matches.
His color was rising and he wouldn't look
at me. "I told them you would be a problem," he said, "when they first promoted
you from the floor. It was obvious to anyone
with eyes. They didn't listen to me." He
found the matches. "We'll mail you your
last paycheck."

"You'll take his word?" I said. "George
Kepler is the worst editor you have. He
takes twice as long as the rest of us."

"You're wasting my time," he said.

There were two more editors at their desks
when I came back to get my things. George
was standing at the side of the room, watch-

13

ing one of the monitors, but he looked over and I stared until he turned away. I packed everything into my purse and a shopping bag I found in the lounge. I had never kept much at my desk anyway. There was a tense silence while I sifted through my papers. The youngest editor, a sweet boy named Carl, was concerned. "Going somewhere?" he said.

"Nice to know you, Carl," I said. It had been. He looked surprised.

And then I was back out on the street again. The awful thing was that it was a beautiful day, one of those slow, rich August afternoons when the light hit the Battery like the inside of a cathedral. I walked slowly, having nowhere I wanted to be, now or for the foreseeable future. A man at a hot dog cart was having an argument with a seagull, which was hopping away with half a pretzel. Two children were racing each other to the railing overlooking the water. The leaves in a stand of little birches were all alight and shivering. I had a pain in my chest, as if I had swallowed too much air. I walked as far as the Staten Island Ferry Terminal and sat on a bench for a long time, doing nothing at all and not seeing much, until it occurred to me that I could smoke. That was something to do. I smoked three or four cigarettes. The six o'clock ferry was leaving, and I got on and went to Staten Island and back, just to feel the sea wind in my hair. I stood at the railing with a crowd of happy visitors taking pictures of the Statue of Liberty and tried to think what to do with myself.

Darkness fell, but made it no easier to imagine going home. I loved my house. I had bought it with cash, all the money from the Argentina job, and I had spent months buying secondhand furniture and painting the windows and trim, learning everything it needed. I couldn't stand the thought of contaminating it with myself, in the state I was in.

Instead I went to the Bracken, my old haunt in the Village. Maxine the bartender was there, making four drinks at once to show off. "Haven't seen you in a while," she said. It was early and the piano player wasn't in yet.

"I was shacked up for a little while," I said.

"That's the trouble," Max said. "Happy girls don't go to bars." She distributed the drinks at the other end of the bar and then came back and made me a gimlet. She had done her mascara in the new way, with the lower lashes so heavy and dark that she looked like a sleepy doll. I told her I liked it, and she turned so she could wink over her shoulder. Max always flirted with me.

"I got fired," I said, experimentally. It had been a year since I stopped my old line of work, but it was still a habit to be close-mouthed.

"Oh, Vera, darling." The eyes went round. She squeezed my forearm. She didn't ask what for, and I didn't tell her.

When the place started to fill up, I left. It was lack of imagination that put me on the B train at West Fourth Street, the train that would take me home, and cowardice that kept me on it, sliding past my own grimy platform, down to Brighton Beach.

CHAPTER 2

I left the luncheonette and walked on the boardwalk. The morning breeze came in from the ocean, lifting my hair off my neck. I liked this beach because the water was so calm. The scythe of the Rockaways protected it from the deep Atlantic currents, and you could bob here peacefully, as if on a Catskills lake. The neat, interlocking planks blurred together in the distance. There was nothing on the sand but a straggling border of seaweed that marked the last high tide. A ship at anchor waited on the horizon.

I had almost no savings. The house had taken everything, and I hadn't made much at the station. I had property taxes to pay, repairs that still had to be made. I walked past shuttered restaurants, overturned terrace tables, a silent gallery of shops whose signs offered hot dogs and fried clams, fountain sodas, banana splits. The abbrevi-

17

ated belfry of a little Catholic church, blotted with pigeons, kept watch behind an ice cream stand.

I did try, Jane. I caught my hair in one hand, fishing in my pocket for bobby pins. Across the water, the dark bulk of New Jersey was lightening as the sun rose. I did try. Just by having you in my house — by saying those things to you, those clever remarks. I made dinner for you. I sat near you and read books. You left clouds of perfume in my bedroom, peeled apples over my sink. If there was something more than that, I couldn't think what it was, what she had wanted from me. She had looked at me searchingly sometimes, early in the morning, and it made me feel sad, diminished. When she was comfortable and happy in the evenings, after a drink or two, she acted sometimes like a child, jostling me with jokes, her voice sugary, and while I could tell I was meant to like this, to be charmed by it, I didn't and wasn't. I went cold instead. Maybe she had sensed that too.

The other woman, where had she come from? Another professor, a graduate student? Jane was invited to dinner parties sometimes with the artists and writers and critics who circulated in her scene, and she would invite me and I usually said no, that

18

I was too tired to talk to strangers or take the train a long way. That looked like a mistake now. I crumpled, and then got angry. Incredible nerve, to accuse me of being cold and then cheat and lie, as if I had no feelings at all. My heart was racing. I pictured her making it with some girl in a cab while I sat at home reading a stupid novel.

The day around me was beginning to look very plain, midmorning on an overcast Thursday late in the summer. I lit a cigarette and turned off the boardwalk onto one of the side streets that led to the elevated tracks of the Q. It was time to go home.

I picked up the newspaper off the front stoop and let myself in. The clock ticked in the kitchen. It was the time of day when the back of the house was the brightest. I made coffee in the Bialetti and turned to the classifieds. In the women's section, columns of ads seeking office girls and waitresses; "pleasant public manner," "well-groomed." Salaries that wouldn't fix the windows or pay the gas bill for the winter. Jane had told me she saw picketers in front of the New York Times Building a few weeks ago because of the sex-segregated classifieds. I hadn't gotten the film-editing job through

19

an ad, of course. I had been hired for a woman's job in the front office and then had insinuated myself into the editing room. That was the only way I had ever managed to make a living: crossing a line bit by bit, as if by accident. I thought of doing it again, starting over in a secretarial position and then casting about to see if I could get something better. But I had no references now. People talked. I couldn't be sure who knew about me. And even if I managed it, they would make undiscussed exceptions for me, do funny things with my title. I wouldn't make much more than the girls answering the phones. I put my head in my hands.

I went into the small back garden and sat for a while, staring at the fence overgrown with morning glories and, beyond it, the windows of the next house. Another day turning. Hours would pass and the yard would grow dark and I wouldn't have spoken to another soul. I thought of my mother. I had seen her in the spring, around Easter time, for the first time in years. I had spent an afternoon and a night in the old family house in Chevy Chase, Maryland, the redbrick colonial with the hedge and flowers. We had been polite to each other. My mother kept sizing me up, always pausing in the doorway of the room I was in before entering, asking discreet questions, as if I were a fellow guest in a hotel. When I was a child, she didn't know what to do with me because I was chaotic and ignorant, like all children; when I was a teenager, she didn't know what to do with me because I was hostile and sad, like most teenagers. The death of my father when I was twelve had left us marooned on separate islands. My appearance in her home in the form of a grown woman caught her off guard, as if it were a disguise I had unfairly put on. She seemed relieved to see me go.

I went through the math again: the windows, the wiring, the gas bill, the taxes.

And then, a trace of an idea. I had been carting around a bundle of Raymond Chandler paperbacks from boardinghouse to apartment to house since my first days in New York. Philip Marlowe, private eye.

Was it so impossible? It was what other ex-spies did. All it took was an office, ads in the paper, referrals. I had the training. I thought of Gerry, my old handler when I worked for the CIA, and laughed. I'd told him I didn't want to do this kind of work anymore. But this would be different.

Half of my remaining money went to pay

for the first and last months' rent for a small office just off Union Square. The office contained a desk with a scarred top, which I covered with a blotter; a stopped clock, which had been screwed directly into the wall and couldn't be removed; and a cast-iron radiator beneath a broad window, the panes of glass old and rippling like water. Through this window I could see the roof of the neighboring building, where a woman came once a day with a basket of laundry to hang up, and part of a synagogue at the end of the block. There was a tiny room in front of the office that the landlord called a "vestibule," which fit one stuffed chair, an end table, and a lamp, and would have to be good enough for a waiting room. The landlord suggested that with some modifications, this outer room could be where my "girl" would sit. I said I would have to be my own girl. He asked what my business was. "Consulting," I said.

By this time, my last check from the television station had arrived by mail, as they said it would, and I cashed it all out to put ads in the *Post* and the *Times,* paying for six weeks up front.

PRIVATE INVESTIGATIONS
SURVEILLANCE —
INQUIRIES OF ALL KINDS

Discreet, professional service
Trained in counterintelligence
English, Spanish & French

Underneath, the number of my telephone answering service, which had instructions to put calls through during the hours I would be in the office. When I first saw the ad printed, the absurdity of the whole idea hit me, but then it ebbed. It was insane to imagine that anyone would hire a woman private investigator, but it was also insane to imagine that any of the other things that had happened to me in the last five years might happen. And things were changing; or at any rate, it looked like they might. Girls only a few years younger than I was seemed louder, freer, in the streets and on the trains. I had read about Haight-Ashbury that summer, and had recoiled. I knew I was supposed to see freedom in the whole enterprise, but I didn't; I saw a whole lot of people acting like children, as if childhood weren't a state of awful helplessness and dependence.

Once the ads were running, I started

spending my days in the office. Easier there than at home. There was work to do, anyway. I gave the wood floor a deep scrubbing, which it obviously hadn't had in a long time, and twisted out the window to clean the outside of the glass. I washed the walls and went around all the gaps and joints of the desk with a pin, levering out the dirt. I brought in a radio so it wouldn't be so quiet. On the third day I got a crank call, and on the fourth day, an obscene one. It was still hot in the mornings; the leaves of a young sycamore just visible over the wall of the synagogue had given up and turned brown. On the fifth day a man with a Long Island accent called and asked me to find out why his wife had left him.

"Your wife?"

"She took the car," he said.

"She stole your car?"

"It's her name on the title. She had it for shopping and summer weekends. Down at the beach, you know." The voice tensed. "But I made the payments."

"How long has she been gone?"

"Six weeks."

"Were you having any troubles? In the marriage?"

"I'd rather tell it to the investigator, miss."

I put my fingers to my temple and closed

24

my eyes. "I'm the investigator, sir."

There was a short laugh and then a pause. "Well," he said. "No, you're joking."

"I'm not. As the advertisement says, I'm trained in counter—"

The line clicked off. I set the phone in the cradle and took a short walk out of the office, down the hall to the service elevator at the back, and then back to the office again. I decided to draw no conclusions whatsoever from what had just happened. I took up my post at the desk again, then changed my mind, went down to the street for a cup of coffee from a cart and the *Daily News,* and came back up. The next day went by the same way. I was becoming very well versed in current events. Then the day after that, and the day after that. Just after I got home in the evening, my next-door neighbor called to say that squirrels were coming from my roof onto his roof and chewing holes into his attic. I told him I didn't know what I could do about it, since the squirrels hadn't asked me for an easement and my efforts to broker a deal with them regarding my own attic had been unsuccessful. He told me that he considered me a bad neighbor, principally because of my weak character, which was creating a squirrel problem that would, in time, stretch up and down the block and doom the neighborhood. I hung up the phone, expressing my regrets and good wishes. I slept badly, thinking about my roof, which had a new leak despite having been fixed just after I bought the house.

The following week, when I received another call from a man asking me to find out why his wife had left him, I explained that he had been lucky to call the office on this particular day because I was a moonlighter who specialized in investigations of ladies, and quoted him an ambitious rate. He accepted my reasoning and even sounded relieved to put the matter in my hands. "She says she's been living with her sister in Astoria," he said. "But I don't believe it. She's never in when I call. I think she's living someplace else with some man."

So I did it: I spent two weeks in my Chevrolet staking out a two-bedroom walk-up in Astoria. The boredom gave rise to strange thoughts, hallucinatory interludes in which I could play out entire alternate lives. When something startled me — a horn blowing, or a child bouncing off the passenger door of my car in pursuit of a rubber ball — I sometimes couldn't remember anything about the previous ten or thirty minutes. On my second Sunday in the car, a break:

the wife paid a visit to the apartment, and I followed her when she left, hanging back a block. She led me to a behemoth apartment building by Corona Park, and I took up my station there for another week, during which time I witnessed her entering the premises with a bearded young man on no fewer than three occasions. I took photos and submitted them to my client. He cried, and then paid my invoice, gathered his hat and rain jacket, and went out desolately into a wet afternoon.

Thoughts of Jane and the other woman were like wasps. I left early that day.

CHAPTER 3

In the next two months I had a couple more jobs like that, which made me dislike myself and other people. I was approached with questions that had a very limited range of possible answers, and none that would make the asker happy. I earned grocery money by upending the minor privacies that people were able to maintain in the busy neighborhoods of Brooklyn and the Bronx. And then one day in December, the telephone on my desk rang and the woman from my service announced a Mr. Ibarra. A low voice came on the line.

"Good morning?" he said.

"Good morning," I answered, and there was a pause that I hated.

"I would like to speak to the investigator," he said.

"Speaking."

There was another hesitation. "You are?"

"Yes."

"You are trained in counterintelligence?"

"That's correct."

"It's unusual." He had a soft accent, and sounded older.

"Yes, sir."

"Well, the matter I'm calling about concerns a child. It's complicated."

"Children are a specialty of mine," I said.

"They are?"

Why not? Perfidious ladies and missing children. "Of course."

"Hmm." He thought it over. "I would need to speak to you in person."

"I'm available now for a consultation." I gave him the address. "Ask the doorman to direct you."

Mr. Ibarra struck me at first like an old country doctor at a funeral — sad, tired, aware of his own importance. He wore a gray suit and was accompanied by his wife, a very small woman with a penetrating gaze only partly diffused by cat-eye glasses. She wore a dark-green wool suit, expensively made; a velvet casque was pinned to her white hair. He stood by absently while she settled herself in the smaller of my two visitor's chairs.

"We're looking for our nephew," he said, when he was also seated. "Our great-nephew."

I spread my hands. "I'm listening."

"Well," he said, as if deciding where to start, "our name is Ibarra. We're Dominican. My wife and I divide our time between our properties in Europe, but most of our family is on the island. The Ibarras are well-known there. Have you ever been to the Dominican Republic?"

"No, I'm afraid I haven't," I said.

"Well. We are a well-known family." He looked like he was trying to think of another way to make me understand this point, but then he went on. "We have a nephew, Dionisio. He and his wife were not on good terms with Trujillo. After Trujillo was shot, they were not on good terms with the ones who came after him. And then two years ago there was the American invasion."

"Yes," I said.

"They were dropping bombs on Santo Domingo. It went on and on. Dionisio and Altagracia were living then at their house in the city with their little son. They couldn't sleep, the boy was having nightmares. Hundreds of people died at the Duarte Bridge. They were afraid of what could happen. They sent him to New York to be safe. An old friend of the family was living here, and they sent him to her. My wife and I

30

were living in Switzerland at the time. The child's name is Félix. He was eleven years old then."

"Who was the friend?" I said.

"A good woman. She had been a servant of the family for many years and had retired. Mrs. Esmeralda Villanueva." He leaned back in the chair. "When the war was over, Joaquín Balaguer became president. Balaguer had all the same grudges as Trujillo. He thought Dionisio had political ambitions. He put him and Altagracia in prison."

I looked at Mrs. Ibarra, but she was unchanging and unobtrusive while her husband spoke. I thought of offering her a cup of tea from the hot plate in the hall, but I couldn't catch her eye.

"No one has heard a word from them," Mr. Ibarra said. "We can't even be sure what prison they are in. And now the boy is missing."

"He's not with the friend anymore?" I said. "Here in New York?"

"No. When we heard Dionisio and Altagracia had been arrested, we flew to the Dominican Republic to help," Mr. Ibarra said. "We went to their estate, spoke to their servants. My niece and nephew had tried to be very discreet, but servants always know.

31

The manager of the house told us that they had sent Félix to Mrs. Villanueva. So we came here to find him. But by the time we arrived, they had both disappeared. The house was empty."

"Who could have taken him?" I said. "Who else knew he was here?"

"We don't know," Mr. Ibarra said.

"They gave him a different name," Mrs. Ibarra said abruptly.

"The housekeeper at the estate said she thought they had taught the boy to go by a false name in New York," said Mr. Ibarra. "But she didn't know what it was. My nephew and his wife told no one." He reached into his jacket and brought out a photograph, which he laid on my desk. The edge had been cut with a pair of scalloped scissors. A young boy, dark eyes, the smoothness of a studio photo; more the idea of a child than a child.

"What a handsome little man," I said, pained. He looked small for his age.

"He's fourteen years old now," Mr. Ibarra said.

"Do you have a more recent photo?"

"No, of course not."

I sighed. "This will be difficult, without even a name."

Mrs. Ibarra was suddenly bawling. Mr.

Ibarra and I both looked at her, startled. "The poor thing," she said, and I gave her a handkerchief from my pocket. Mr. Ibarra leaned toward me, around his hunched, weeping wife. "We'll pay a retainer," he said.

I went that same afternoon to the address they gave me for Esmeralda Villanueva, confidante and nursemaid to the Ibarra family for forty years. She lived at 72 Webb Street in Sheepshead Bay. I drove my rattling Chevrolet there and parked at the end of Avenue X. Sheepshead Bay was a little Venice of clapboard houses, interrupted by pockets of woods; as I walked I came across the water without warning, an ordinary street dead-ending in a cluster of sailboats. I doubled back, past a delicatessen and a high-fenced lot behind which I heard the shuffling and snorting of horses. The house on Webb Street was battered but tidy, a wood-frame box with colorless siding, perched at the edge of the water. A curtain lifted and dropped next door, and I made a show of going up and knocking on the door, standing expectantly there on the porch, knocking again. The front door of the neighbor's house opened.

"There's nobody living there," said a woman in a housedress.

I had put on a hat and gloves before I left, to give the impression of a saleslady. "I'm looking for Mrs. Villanueva."

"She died." The woman leaned back in the doorway, with some satisfaction. "It was terrible."

"Oh, no." I covered my mouth with my hand, a gesture that surprised me by being genuine. "What happened?"

"Are you from the city?"

"No, no. Avon," I said. "She was a customer."

"It was a heart attack. I saw them wheel her out."

"What about her boy? Poor thing — now I can't think of his name . . ."

"Bobby, I think it was."

"He's a sweet boy. Bobby Villanueva, was it? What happened to him?"

The woman was edging back inside. "Couldn't tell you," she said. "We weren't on friendly terms. There was a tree in her yard that leaned into mine."

"A tree?"

"It's cut down now," the woman said, and let the door fall shut behind her.

I briefly considered knocking on her door to ask more questions, but the guise of a saleslady wouldn't support it. Instead I glanced up and down the empty street, then leaned close and looked through the window, shading the glass with my hands. A living room crowded with furniture. No one had come to clear it all away. I stepped down off the porch and picked my way around to the side yard, past a stack of bricks under a tarp and a cluster of garbage cans. Through the windows, more furnished rooms, untouched. In the backyard, a stump. I imagined the triumph of the neighbor, watching the tree come down. I walked back to my car and sat for a while, thinking. Shaken that what had looked like intrigue was only an ordinary awful death, which suggested awful, simple explanations for the disappearance of the boy — that he'd been left alone, and had been taken advantage of.

I lay awake for a long time that night with Félix on my mind. Who could he know in this city? Where could he have gone? Or was he taken? Trujillo had had CIA backing. President Balaguer had it now, having landed on top at the conclusion of the Dominican Civil War. Had they found Félix, even out there in Sheepshead Bay, his every connection to his family broken or concealed?

At two o'clock in the morning it all came

to me at once. *Are you from the city?* the woman had said. I hadn't been thinking the right way. I turned over and slept soundly.

In the morning I took the telephone directory to the kitchen table and found the number for the Bureau of Child Welfare. A faint secretarial voice answered at the main switchboard. "Child Welfare," she said. "How may I direct your call?"

"I'm looking for a child who was taken into care," I said. "He had no relatives."

"You're inquiring about adoption, ma'am?"

"No, I'm looking for a child. A fourteen-year-old boy."

"Your child was removed? Speak to your caseworker, ma'am."

"No. He's not my child. I'm a neighbor. He was living with his grandmother and she died. I just heard. The city took him away. I'm trying to find out where they took him."

"Hold, please."

I waited. The vine that had traveled across the top of the window over the kitchen sink was leafless now, and I could see the sky above the house at the back of mine.

There was a click, and then a firmer voice. "Intake unit."

"I'm looking for a child I know," I said.

"He was living with his grandmother, but she died a few months ago and I haven't been able to learn where he is now. I heard the city took him in."

"How do you know this child, ma'am?"

"I was a neighbor. I thought he might like to see a friendly face. I feel terrible about his grandmother."

There was a short silence. "We don't share that kind of information, outside of the family."

"But he doesn't have any family."

She sighed. "What's the name?"

"Bobby Villanueva. His grandmother was Esmeralda Villanueva. She died a few months ago. He's fourteen years old."

"Robert Villanueva?"

"Probably. But I'm not sure, she only ever called him Bobby."

"You're not sure of the name? Ma'am, do you know how many children there are in foster care in this city?"

"I'm sorry." I searched around for a feeling that would be useful. "I just couldn't live with myself if I didn't try to get ahold of him. She was all he had. They lived at 72 Webb Street in Sheepshead Bay — does that help?"

"Well," she said. "I can check the log for that address. That's all I can do. But they

37

don't always get the addresses right in the log."

"I would so appreciate it."

"Hold, please."

For ten minutes, and then fifteen, and then twenty, I listened to the uneasy hum on the line. Tethered to the wall by the telephone cord, I made coffee and thought about toast. It hardly seemed worth the effort. My appetite was an idea I'd had once and reconsidered. The woman came back on the line.

"There's no one by that name, but there's a boy with that address who came in on the sixth of September."

That put some color in my cheeks. "What was the name?"

"Robert Calendar. He was taken by Catholic Family Services."

"Taken?"

"Children don't stay here. This is intake. They get transferred. I'll give you the phone number." She read it off. "Is there anything else?"

"No, thank you."

It had to be the same boy. I called the number for Catholic Family Services and explained what I was after.

"We have children all across the city," said an irritated woman in the administrative office. "We run eleven programs. You don't know where he is?"

"I'm so sorry," I said. "If you'll just give me the numbers for the eleven programs, I'll call them myself."

To my surprise, she did this, reading them off in a tone that began to slide toward remorse. Once I had them all written down she said apologetically, "If he's fourteen, he's probably at Saint Jerome."

"What's Saint Jerome?"

"The campus up in Westchester. That's where they take all the older boys."

"Thank you."

I called Saint Jerome and got a secretary on the line.

"He would have come in just a few months ago," I said. "He was picked up by the Bureau of Child Welfare on the sixth of September."

"There's no one here by that name."

I took a deep breath, to control my voice. "Was any fourteen-year-old Dominican boy admitted to your program in the last three months?"

"I'm not playing detective, ma'am. There's no Calendar boy here. I've just looked at the registration list."

"His grandmother's name —"

"There are four hundred boys here. You're

39

wasting my time."

I tried the other numbers I'd been given, just in case. No one had ever heard of Robert Calendar, or knew the addresses the boys had come from, or even the boroughs. At the last three numbers on the list, the telephone only rang and rang.

When I finally hung up, the winter sun was coming in strongly through the back windows and the quiet of the kitchen had resolved into buzzing and ticking. I felt tense. I made oatmeal and ate half of it. I walked absently in circles, tidying up, and then stood still and closed my eyes. An old smell was in my nose: ammonia and boiled meat. The grates bolted over the windows. The powdered eggs. Waking at three o'clock in the morning, not knowing where I was, and then remembering.

I had taken my mother's car one bad night when I was seventeen and driven it to my aunt's house in Baltimore, and my mother had called the police. I spent thirty days in juvenile detention at the Maryland Youth Center. Many of my fellow delinquents were released to reformatories that were run by Child Welfare, to wait out the months or years until they reached the age of majority and could be left to their own devices. It was a transitional place, the Maryland Youth

40

Center, a locked room where we waited while the world decided what to do with us. My mother sent me to a boarding school once my thirty days were up. I never lived at home again.

Jane and I were together six months. The Maryland Youth Center was one of the things I had never told her. There were others. For her part, she had taken a deep breath the third time we went out and told me everything she could think of about herself, her mother and father moving from rental house to rental house in the frozen counties around Albany, a little brother in the army, two collie mixes napping in a childhood kitchen. Getting lost on a Girl Scout camping trip and coming home so covered in poison ivy that they had to take her to the hospital. High school boyfriends. She sent her parents friendly letters from the city every two weeks, saw them three times a year. Never quite told them a lie. They never asked about men.

She didn't understand why I hardly spoke to my mother. All her life, she had managed other people easily. The difficulty between me and Elizabeth Kelly looked to Jane like a problem that could be solved with the same cheery rigidity she had used when her

41

landlord had seen her coming up the back stairs with me late one night and had threatened to terminate her lease. She had gone down to the lobby with him and spent twenty minutes politely refusing to understand what he was saying, until he gave up in embarrassment and frustration. He never raised the issue again, and we were more discreet after that.

I went for a walk to think over my problem with the Bureau of Child Welfare. The day was dense with rain that wouldn't fall, the sky the color of ash, and Prospect Park was beautiful in that kind of weather, the brambles strung with beads of cold water, the branches of the oaks black against the sky at the edge of the Nethermead. At that time of day the park was haunted by solitary women in head scarves, walking rangy dogs — a category of women I thought of as The Widows. I took a path that looped back and forth across a long, motionless pond. The woods were quiet.

In Argentina I had needed information about a group of students, and I had been given a brief to infiltrate, which meant, in that case, paying the international student fee at the university and making myself their friend. When you have little to go on, you have to just go where the action is and hang around until something happens.

I still had a fake driver's license that I had kept in my wallet during my first years in New York, when I was going out dancing and didn't want the police to get my name if there was a raid. If you showed them identification, they might send you home; if you refused, they would make you sit for a day or two in the Tombs out of spite, and once they got your real name they would put it in the blotter. My fake said my name was Rose Davies. I remembered the man who'd sold it to me, a little guy from Flushing who hung around with speed freaks but wasn't one. I wondered if he could supply social security cards as well. I was going to need one, because I was applying for a job.

43

CHAPTER 4

The jewel in the crown of Catholic Family Services was Saint Jerome's School for Boys, a winding drive to a hidden campus of white buildings on a hill in the town of Oakwood, New York, site of a Revolutionary War defeat and an ancient ferry landing. I took the train from Grand Central to Westchester County. On a historical society plaque at the Oakwood station, I read that the town was also home to the ruins of a barn and meeting house that had belonged to a celibate utopian commune, which had eased into extinction for obvious reasons in 1882. They had raised sheep, sold wool, and fired bricks. I checked my hair in a mirror compact and used a tissue to edge away lipstick that had crept too far.

I had called Mr. Ibarra a few days before to tell him that I suspected Félix had been picked up by Child Welfare, and suggested he make inquiries, since he was family. He

44

tried, but got nowhere. There was no one listed anywhere under the name Félix Ibarra, and when he said the boy might be using another name, the officials on the other end became suspicious and evasive. He stuttered with frustration when he told me on the telephone.

The campus was a mile and a half up a steep road. A vanload of boys passed and jeered at me while I climbed it, and I looked into half a dozen teenage faces for an instant; they were delighted and angry, and then gone. I was warm when I got to the top of the hill. A sign next to a guard's booth at the school gate made the T in SAINT JEROME into a large cross, which split in half a line of praise for the generosity of the governor that ran across the bottom of the board. I explained my reason for visiting to the man in the booth, who tipped slowly off his stool and came out to open the gate. I walked up the drive to the administration building.

At the front desk, just inside the foyer, a secretary was changing the ribbon on her typewriter.

"I'm looking for work," I said. It was less than a week to Christmas, and an artificial tree stood behind the secretary, the boughs frosted with artificial snow.

"What kind of work?" she said.

"I've been a caseworker and an aide."

"Have you seen the listings?" she said.

"I haven't."

"I've got them here." She pulled a folder from a drawer. "You can sit there on the bench."

I took the listings to the bench. It was a sheaf of St. Jerome's help-wanted ads, mimeographed from the pages of the Westchester papers. A dozen at least. Cooks, porters, caseworkers, social workers, clerks, guards.

"There's quite a lot," I ventured.

"People come and they go," the secretary said.

I fished my résumé out of my bag and chose the ad for the caseworker. A woman whose stockings were coming down blustered in, her hair wild. "Margaretta," she said to the secretary. "Mother of God, those boys in Cottage 4."

"You're not supposed to be in there without Chambers."

"Tell that to my supervisor."

"Ha. If I could find him," said the secretary.

"They blocked the door with a bunk bed. They want to keep me out, let them."

46

"You're not going in there without Chambers."

"Your lips to God's ear."

I was hovering, holding out the résumé and the ad. "Caseworker, please. I'd like to apply."

The women both turned to look at me, taking their time about it. I thought there might be a way for me to adopt their stance, to join their side. A few comments sprang to mind, things to say about the jobs that I was pretending to have had, the facilities and institutions listed on the fabricated résumé in my hand. But from the stillness of their faces when they looked at me, I could see that I shouldn't try.

The secretary took the papers and read them. The woman with her stockings bunched up in her shoes leaned against the wall and began to smooth her hair with her fingers.

"I'll give this to the residential director," the secretary said. "But he'll say yes. We've been very short. Be ready to come back after Christmas."

The triumph I felt about my success in this venture had begun to fade by the time the train pulled into Grand Central Terminal, and when I had the idea to go to the

Bracken, I didn't try all that hard to resist it. The weather had turned ugly by then, and though it was just five thirty, time for the office girls, the bar was quiet. The lights had not yet been dimmed for the evening. I could see the places in the floor where the nails stood out from boards that had been worn down by dancing. The row of Moroccan lanterns over the bar looked cheery. Max the bartender was smoking, leaning back against the cash register. She had a nice way of doing nothing without looking bored. She nodded when I came in, folding a fifty-cent umbrella I had just been forced by necessity to buy at the deli on the corner. My coat was spotted with rain.

"I was starting to think they'd dropped the bomb and nobody told me," she said.

"You've got customers," I said. There were a couple of women in a booth.

"They're sculptures. They came with the place."

I laughed. "A gimlet, please."

"I'm going to promote you off the bottom shelf today, just because." She uncapped a bottle of Tanqueray.

"You're much too kind." I watched her work. The hem at her neckline had come unstitched on one side, and the fabric was creeping up. I wondered if she lived in a boardinghouse, like I used to. Some girls in the scene still lived at home with their mothers and fathers. But no, I thought. If she lived with her mother, her collar would be fixed.

"I think I got a new job today," I said.

"Oh yeah? That's terrific." She took her own glass out from a low shelf. "Where?"

"A reform school up in Westchester."

"That's some commute."

"I suppose so. But beggars can't be choosers."

"So they say. You're a teacher?"

"Something like that."

She looked at me as if expecting me to go on, but I didn't.

"Cheers to those who have the patience for it," she said finally, and then went to the other end of the bar to attend to one of the women who had just surfaced from the booth.

Something was wrong in the shadows in front of my house. I stepped back where I couldn't be seen. The street was lined with leaning trees, and the shadows of the street-lights made things complicated, but some-one was there. I crossed to number 117 and turned to look. A figure was huddled at the top of my stoop with arms around knees, smoking. It was Jane. She always sat like a kid, folded up. I was pleased, then angry, then ashamed of having been pleased. I crossed the street again, making myself obvious now. She stood up. I needed to get the light over my front door fixed; I couldn't have this dark space there for people to crouch in. It needed to be rewired — that was another bill. I stopped at the bottom of the stoop, as if she owned the place and I had come to sell her a vacuum cleaner. "Hello," I said.

"Vera," she said. "I'm sorry to show up like this. I've been trying to call but I never seem to get you."

"You never do." She was standing the way she did when she was nervous, with her knees together and her feet pigeon-toed. She was small and round, with hair almost as curly as mine, a blushing dynamo if she felt like dancing, unconvincing at contrition and apologies and everything else she was likely to do tonight.

"I left some — I'm sorry. I want to apologize," she said.

"On the stoop?" I had withdrawn. I could feel it happening; it was almost physical.

"Well, if you want. Or I could come in."

I went up and let her in. The house was cold; since I lost my job I had been turning

50

down the boiler whenever I left. I wished I hadn't today. I wished the house were warm and inviting and I could refuse to ask her to sit down, or maybe I wished that I could make her a pot roast and wrap her in a blanket. I dropped my keys on the hall table and walked into the kitchen. She could follow me if she wanted. She followed me.

"I left my notes," she said.

"What notes?" Under the kitchen light I could see that she had dyed her hair again. It was red, and some of the curl had gone out of it. I had always thought she had the face of an English governess, milky and small featured, freckled but serious. When she had a meeting with the dean she always penciled her eyebrows in. She said she felt like she wasn't quite there otherwise.

"For the *Comparative Review* paper," she said.

"I would have mailed them to you."

She was wringing her hands. Her face was pink from the cold. "I wanted to talk to you."

She had no business looking so embarrassed when I was the humiliated one. I was the one who wasn't enough. When would this scalding stop?

"What did you want to say?" I said.

"That I'm sorry. For the way I behaved.

With — with Louise."

"That's her name? Why are you coming over to my house and telling me her name?"

She went on. "I didn't mean to lie to you. I really never did. It happened bit by bit and then it was — happening. I'm so sorry."

"When did it start?"

"When did it — well . . . I —"

"When did you start to lie to me?"

She looked alarmed. She dropped her gaze to her shoes. "In July, I guess it was."

We'd had a beautiful summer together. I had thought. My ribs felt like I was stuck in a girdle. "In July," I repeated. "When we went to Montauk."

"It was just after that." She looked pained. My eyes were wet. I turned around quickly, took a glass off a shelf, put it down.

"It doesn't matter now anyway," she said. "It fell apart. It wasn't much to start with. I'm so stupid, Vera. I don't know what's the matter with me."

"It's all right," I said, which didn't make any sense.

"It's not all right. I've been a pig." She was crying in earnest now, her shoulders shaking. "She borrowed money from me, Vera. God knows what she was doing with hers. I covered three months of her rent up front, and then she said she had to think

52

things over and got on a train to Montreal. I even took an advance on my salary. I feel like the stupidest person in the world." Her eyes were swollen and she looked light-headed, tentative. I pulled the kitchen chair out for her and brushed her hair out of her wet face. She rested her head against my waist and I let her. "Fools rush in," she said. "Sometimes I think you're the only person I've ever met who's not a fool. Couldn't be one if you tried."

"Please," I said.

"It's true."

"Come on," I said. It was a sad idea, to never come unstuck from yourself. Her tears were leaking through my dress. "Look, I think you should have some tea and whiskey."

"All right," she said.

I wondered if she had eaten. She sometimes forgot. While the kettle was coming to a boil, I went to the living room and turned the thermostat up from where I had left it all day. In the depths of the house the radiators kicked on, whistling.

Once she had had her hot toddy and a sandwich, she pulled herself together. I went and got her papers for her. It felt strange, retrieving them from the second bedroom, which she had used as an office during the long weekends she spent at my place. They were just where she had left them, shuffled together and held down with a dictionary on the desk in the corner. I had left them there because it hurt to move them, and it was as if, by coming back, she had kindly offered an end to the spell that bound me from entering this room. I looked at the first page. I couldn't make much sense of it. I hadn't been to school the way Jane had. I wondered if I had been successful in hiding from her the way she intimidated me, with her mountains of books and chummy arguments about style. She came from the college livid sometimes; she had published more than anyone in her tier and was still only a lecturer. All the tenured places went to men. We had fought about it once. I had called her naive.

When I came down with the papers, Jane was washing her mug and plate in the sink.

"You don't have to do that," I said. I had gotten very tired on the trip back down the stairs. She didn't answer. I watched her set the dishes aside and dry her hands.

"Can I use your telephone?" she said. "I think I'll be extravagant and call a cab."

"Of course." I pointed to it, although she knew where it was.

I waited with her on the stoop. "You know,

I lost my job," I said, after thinking about it for a long time.

"No!" I could see her trying to make out my expression in the dark. "What happened?"

I started to clear my throat but only made a humming noise. "Kepler heard me on the phone with you."

She said nothing at first and I regretted having spoken. She would think I wanted her to feel bad about it. I didn't. It was my own fault, or Kepler's. Mr. Anderson's, for being such a coward. It would be hard to replace me. I shifted, not wanting to catch her eye, and then remembered the cigarette I had put behind my ear and lit it. She put her arm around me and squeezed my shoulder.

"That's hideous," she said.

"Yes, well," I said. Her cab arrived, and her hand slipped away. I watched her go down the steps and cross the sidewalk, light on her feet, like a bird.

As predicted, the residential director at Saint Jerome called on Thursday and asked if I could start on Tuesday, which was the day after Christmas. I agreed. I was pleased and eager to begin, and it wasn't all because of the case. Distractions were welcome.

After the call, I went back to the business of the week, which was finding a way to survive the holiday, once again.

In the end, I fell back on an old Christmas strategy: matinees all afternoon at a movie theater on Houston Street — *Doctor Dolittle,* then *Fitzwilly,* then *The Graduate,* and then, why not, I waited in my seat until they played *The Graduate* again. Afterward I went to a place in the Lower East Side that served beef burgundy, which I ordered and then ate with two glasses of beer. The waiter winked when he brought the drinks, as if to say that he was letting me get away with something untoward.

I slept poorly that night, as I always did before the first day at a new job. I kept having twitchy nightmares about trains I couldn't catch. I gave up and got out of bed at five thirty, choosing a sober outfit: a wool skirt, blocky shoes. I got the paper off the stoop and read it for a while in the kitchen. All bad news. ALLIED CEASEFIRE ENDS IN VIETNAM – BOMBING RESUMES. It was a relief when the time came to walk to the B train.

It was a drizzling gray morning in Oakwood, New York. I was checked in by the same secretary I had seen before, and directed to a hot, narrow office with a stack of forms to fill out, then shown to a large, tiled room filled with desks. The windows were open, letting in the damp air and letting out the smell of bleach from still-wet floors.

"This is the casework office," said the secretary. "The girls do their own typing. You can type?"

"I can type." Through the cantilevered windows I could see the school building. White columns across the front affected to hold up a pediment depicting St. Jerome in concrete relief, engaged in some nonspecific act of charity with a group of children. Behind the school, a lawn shocked brown by the winter ended in a tangle of bare trees and undergrowth. In the distance, the silver of the Hudson River, soft with fog this morning.

"Take an empty desk," the secretary said. "But make sure it *is* empty."

My supervisor was Mrs. Allen. Mrs. Allen would be in at ten o'clock. I chose a desk and put my pen and pad in the top drawer. The building was quiet. I could hear footsteps from time to time, and female voices raised in joking or complaining tones, but I couldn't tell where they were coming from. I hadn't expected it to be quiet. The Maryland Youth Center had filled my head as soon as I walked in the gate that morning, and that had been a noisy place, even when the matrons managed to hector and punish us into silence. Our shoes echoed and squeaked, we elbowed and thumped each other, we were always just contained. The breakfast trays were deafening as they came through the dishwasher's window in the dining room, the staff telephone was always ringing to no effect, the immense soup pots in the kitchen went off like gongs. Finally I remembered that it was the day after Christmas and the boys who weren't home on leave were probably sleeping late, off school for the week.

Mrs. Allen swept in, wearing a belted raincoat and galoshes, at 9:55 AM.

"You're the new one?" she said. "Miss Davies?"

"Yes." I had long since finished my paperwork and had been staring out the window at the lawn like it was the sea off Nantucket. I watched her maneuver into her desk, which was the largest and the closest to the window, and had a trio of potted ferns across the front that bobbed and trembled as she dropped her things on the blotter. She was thick in the arms and legs, muscular, with a matter-of-fact face. She looked about fifty. "We're giving you the boys in Cottage 9," she said. "Mrs. Minsky will give you their files."

CHAPTER 5

There were twelve boys in Cottage 9, ranging in age from fourteen to sixteen. Down the spine of each binder file ran a typed label that gave the boy's blood type and stated that he was or was not allergic to penicillin: a large YES or NO. On the first page of each file was a photo of the child, and underneath, a description of his body: his hair and eye and skin color, *dark-skinned, yellow, olive, ruddy, freckled, fair, white.* His height and weight, distinguishing marks. *Keloid scars on left shoulder and back; burn marks on backs of both hands; puncture scarring on right cheek; acne scars on face and upper back.* Race: *black, mulatto, white, white ethnic, Spanish, Jewish, Oriental.* I longed for the specificity blotted out by *Spanish.* How many Dominicans?

The room filled with caseworkers. A cheery young Puerto Rican woman, who had a diploma from the graduate program in social work at Hunter College framed on the bit of wall closest to her desk, took me to a supply closet and a huge set of taupe filing cabinets and explained all the documentation. Her name was Gladys. She pulled form after form in triplicate from cabinets and mail bins screwed to the wall. "These are every week," she said, placing a paper gently on the stack in my hands at the end of each sentence. "These are every month. These are every quarter. These are only once every six months, good thing, ha ha! Because the first time I did one, it took me two days. You want to keep your old ones and copy over some of the information. And these are yearly. These are incident reports. Remember to keep copies! Because the review board can take up to six months to look at them and then they call you up with a question and you can hardly remember what happened! These are supply requests. These are external incident reports. These are police reports. These are missing child reports. These are injury reports. These are morning rounds. You won't have to do those but once a month when you're on call. These are evening rounds. These are behavior logs. These are leave logs. These are family visitation logs."

"My goodness," I said finally.

"You know what they say," she said. "If it's not documented, it didn't happen."

"Do they say that?"

"Mrs. Allen certainly does!" She walked back to her desk and I followed her. "You have to make sure you see each boy once a week. You'll see them more often than that, but at least once a week you have to document it. Use the casework visit form. You say what you talked about, how they looked, whether they behaved or not. You talk to the family at least once a month. It can be on the telephone, but then you have to use the telephone form. If the boy is allowed to go home for visits, you have to inspect the home once every six months. That keeps you busy, with twelve boys! Request the train tickets ahead of time from Mrs. Minsky. She keeps a bundle in the reception desk."

"How do you like it here?" I said.

She looked me over. I could see her deciding something, although whether it was about me or not, I wasn't sure. She leaned forward. The other caseworkers and social workers were busy, and the room was filled with a buzz of low conversation, of drawers opening and closing on tight tracks, the casters of wheeled chairs squealing and spinning.

"Is this work political for you?" she said.

I often felt that because of my past work, I knew both too much and too little about politics: that my original naivete had been replaced wholesale and overnight by a congealed cynicism, which only grew thicker the more I read. I looked curiously at Gladys. "I don't know," I said.

"It is for me," she said. "And that's why I chose this place, and that's also why it drives me crazy."

I hadn't met many women who spoke this way, at least not outside the circles that Jane traveled in. Gladys's look was entirely square — hair curled and sprayed, nails painted pink. I glanced around at the room of similarly dressed women.

"Mrs. Allen said you can speak Spanish," she said. "Where are you from?"

"Washington, DC," I said.

"Your parents, though?"

"Montana and Texas."

"You're not Hispanic?"

"No," I said. "I just studied it in school."

"We'll test you," she said, smiling. "Some of these boys don't talk like they teach you in school."

I read through the charts of the boys on my caseload. They were filled with reports from reform schools and juvenile detention centers and the agencies that sent social workers into homes, social workers who wrote down the contents of the refrigerator and the pantry, noted the fire exits, made lists of items for remediation: *lock broken, window won't open, back door blocked, plaster falling, not enough beds.* Some of the boys were truant and had been arrested for thefts or fights and had arrived at Saint Jerome by the same route that took me to the Maryland Youth Center: the courts. They were boys who couldn't be managed and wouldn't stay home. Others had no one left to look after them. Two were orphans; more had one missing parent and one listed as *ill* or *unsuitable. Unsuitable* led back through its own chain of documents, into a past that appeared unknowable and confused even if it spanned only a few years — court orders and home visitation papers in which the spelling of names changed repeatedly, the order of deaths and arrests and other cataclysms was disputed, addresses were only partly legible in faded third-page triplicate. Documents that showed the boys' official movements from the custody of one entity to another, wandering and backtracking through the state of New York, were interrupted by periodic examinations of their bodies. Heights and weights advanced as I turned the pages. Teeth were filled or extracted. Haircut allowances were requested, mislaid, requested again. There were inventories of their possessions, lists of their clothing: *knit hat, oxford shirt, four pairs socks, shoes (tennis), shoes (leather/church).*

There had been girls at the Maryland Youth Center, I thought, whose inventories would have been as brief as this. At that age I'd had a mahogany bedroom set, a record player, a closet full of good shoes and coats, although of course none of that came with me. I had been broke later, and it made the world into a constant abrasion. I remembered what another girl at MYC had said to me when I was told I was being transferred to the Barrington School at the end of my thirty days: "It must be nice to have money." The girls who didn't had come to places like this. Had Félix been old enough to understand, at eleven, what his family really was? I thought of *A Little Princess:* the orphaned child whose parent returns, the poor child who turns out to be rich. The death that was only a misunderstanding.

When my own father died, after a week in the hospital, no one told me for two days. My mother didn't know how to say it. The hours ticked by. Since the day he was taken away, I had been playing a brutal and exacting game with myself: if I didn't do this, didn't do that, then he would come home. I was still playing when she finally came to tell me the news.

As I worked my way through the filing cabinets, learning the organizational system, I tried to guess where the master lists of residents might be. I wished again that I had a more recent photograph of Félix.

Mr. Ibarra's first check had cleared. It might all be going all right.

It wasn't until three o'clock that I was offered a chance to meet the boys of Cottage 9. I was led there by a somber man in his fifties named Mr. Jenkins, who wore a coat and tie. I followed him down a broad driveway and along a brick path. "They should be studying," he said as we approached. "Final exams are after the break." It was a brick building, an odd size; a tar-shingled roof angled down over small windows. Mr. Jenkins knocked once and pushed open the door. "Muster, gentlemen," he called out. "You've got a new worker."

It was an open hall lined with bunks. There were two desks in front, and a boy in glasses who was sitting at one, holding a sandwich, looked up at me. "What happened to Miss Flores?"

"Nothing happened to her. She's in her office. This is Miss Davies, she's the new caseworker." He called out again. "I said muster up, boys."

A few boys dangled from their bunks and then dropped to the floor like cats, ignoring the ladders bolted to the frames. I watched twelve boys assemble. They did so languidly, but didn't take long. A kind of remote compliance. I was embarrassed and couldn't say why. Maybe because they had been through this scene so many more times than I had. *People come and they go,* the secretary had said.

"Hello," I said. "I'm Miss Davies. It's really nice to meet you."

"Say hello, Cottage 9," said Mr. Jenkins.

"Hello," said Cottage 9. A smaller boy near the wall smiled broadly, but the rest did not.

"Michael, where are your glasses?" Mr. Jenkins said.

"I don't know, Mr. Jenkins." Michael was tall and brown skinned, a pencil line of mustache growing in, his hair parted and combed back.

"You don't know? Those glasses were new."

"They were from last year."

67

"Last year is new, Michael. When did you lose them?"

"A couple of days ago."

"That's not answering the question."

"It was on Friday, I believe, sir."

"Where did you go on Friday?"

"Just to school and the cafeteria and back to here."

"No home visit?"

Two other boys in the line abruptly shifted their weight and looked upward.

"No, sir, I didn't get a pass."

"Oh, that's right." Mr. Jenkins glanced at me. I began to wonder if this interrogation was for my benefit, and if so, what I was supposed to get from it. I could see that the boys didn't want to cross him, at least not to his face. I could see that they came when he told them to. "How many weekends did you lose?"

"Three, sir."

"Next time, might not seem worth it."

"Might not, sir."

"Well." Mr. Jenkins crossed his arms. "I want you all to behave yourselves for Miss Davies."

They said nothing. I smiled again. Mr. Jenkins turned and let himself out, and I clasped my hands. "Can you all tell me your names?"

68

Michael looked down at me from his great height, with a narrow gaze that I now understood to be myopic. "I'm Michael," he said, and the boys all laughed.

"So I heard," I said.

The rest were Tommy, Carlos, Anthony, Emil, Yakov, Frankie, Clarence, Clark, James, Randall, Cesar. I said my own fake name twelve times, shook twelve hands. There were obscure currents in the room around Michael, around the missing glasses and the forfeited home-visit pass. The feeling of undercover work was coming back to me: the way of being lightly balanced, ready to break in any direction, follow the lead of any person in the room. "He gave you a hard time," I hazarded to Michael.

"That's just Mr. J, miss," he said neutrally.

"Well. It was nice to meet you all," I said. As I left, I sensed the rearrangement of bodies and expressions that always followed the exit of an adult from any room full of adolescents.

I sat by the window on the way home, watching the river darkening beneath its feldspar cliffs. Now and then I saw cargo ships, striated with rust, headed north. I loved this and every river in a way that was hard to articulate, even to myself. Water

69

makes a perfect line. It had been a dim, rainy day, and the river was dim too, softening now into darkness, passing villages where the lights were coming on. I knew it was very deep and very cold, and the current was strong. Here and there, small jetties traced with lights ventured into it and stopped.

Jane had this feeling about the ocean. The ocean had always been impersonal to me, but it settled her. She had been very happy in Montauk that summer, those four days we had spent in a rental house two sandy blocks from the beach, packing sandwiches in wax paper in the mornings, her freckled shoulders bare, a handkerchief tied over her hair to keep it from tangling in the breezes that swept in from the Long Island Sound.

I thought about the Bracken again while the train found its track in the diverging and converging lines beneath Grand Central. But I had another early day ahead of me. Better not to. It would be another forty minutes before I was home, and then I would make a mash out of whatever I could find in the refrigerator, have some of my own whiskey, and put the television on.

CHAPTER 6

Michael had been marked late for curfew on Wednesday night, arriving at the cottage for check-in with the evening staff at 9:37 PM. And on Thursday morning in the cafeteria, he had his glasses back. I had been asked to supervise breakfast, and I was standing at the back, where I could see the shuffling boys moving down the line with their trays.

He was a leader, I could see that. He said less, moved less quickly than the rest, and yet was always flanked by friends. I had looked over his chart again. His mother worked for the postal service and said she could no longer have him in the house. He had stolen twenty dollars from her purse, he had stayed out all night too many times, she was tired of calling the police to go looking for him. His father was dead, KIA in Korea when Michael was small. An older brother in Connecticut had kept him for a

71

month here and there but had just had twin babies of his own and didn't have the space to put him up when he fought with their mother anymore. He'd been arrested in Central Park for truancy in September and then sent here, not for the first time. He was five feet eleven inches tall, weighed one hundred thirty-eight pounds, and was allergic to milk and pineapple.

His best friend was Cesar. Cesar was short and strong, and spoke with incredible speed and intricacy in a soft Bronx accent. He was funny, although I could catch only half of what he said; the other boys would have gone to war for him. Both boys were evasive and deferential to me, and in the three days I had spent on campus neither had answered any question I asked with more than three words in a row, of which one was invariably "miss." Some of the younger boys, on the other hand, scowled in silence, or edged close to the hostile, flirtatious style of grown men calling after girls on the street. It was such an obvious performance that it made them seem too small for their own clothes, as if they had been badly costumed for a play. Gladys said, "They think if you get too comfortable and stay, their social worker will leave."

"Why?"

"Because sometimes that's what happens. The good workers feel bad leaving when we're short-staffed, so they wait until another position gets filled before they give notice."

"Does she want to leave?" Their social worker was Miss Flores, who had been there two years.

"Who knows?"

I had gotten a look at the admissions lists by saying I needed to find somebody's mother's maiden name, but even that excuse seemed unnecessary. No one was particularly interested in what records I needed or why. The reports we had to write asked for reams of information like that, and the caseworkers were always paging through old files, looking persecuted. The admissions list was a huge logbook, bound in vinyl that was pressed to look like leather, housed on a shelf in a storage closet filled with identical logs that went back twenty years. I found the one marked *Aug–Oct 1967* and paged through to September. On September 20 there was a Robert Candelario, age fourteen, admitted and assigned to Cottage 4. His date of birth was wrong, by a month and a day. Could it have been him? A misspelling, or an alias slipping, or only a coincidence that would waste my time? I read through the logs up to the present, to see if Candelario had been marked as discharged or transferred, but his name didn't appear again. If he wasn't discharged or transferred, he should have been present. And yet the population list, which was updated every day with the name of every boy currently in the charge of St. Jerome's, and which was posted on the wall in the guard booth and on a bulletin board in the staff room, did not include his name.

I was considering all this while I watched Michael, who looked happier and more alert with his glasses on. I saw another boy point to his own face and then to Michael's, as if in congratulations, and they both laughed. According to the logs, Michael had been on and off this campus four times in the past three years. If anyone was likely to know who had come and gone among the boys, it was him.

There was a common room for the boys between the cafeteria and the library. It was a mirror image of the staff lounge in the administration building, although the boys were likely unaware of that, since the staff guarded access to the lounge as if it were a nightclub. Both rooms were tiled, with bright overhead lights and windows that looked out on the downward-sloping lawns and the edge of the woods where deer sometimes appeared at dusk. Both contained the same battered yellow pine furniture, modular for stacking and heavily varnished. Against one wall, there was a sink, a cabinet gritty with powdered creamer, and a counter with a coffeepot. The boys used the common room to play cards and took turns being caught smoking. Because of this habit, the windows were always cranked open a few inches, and the room was cold and damp from the air that rose up the hill from the river.

After the second time in my first week that cigarettes had been confiscated from ninth graders in the common room, I was assigned to sit there for the two hours after classes let out and before dinner was served. I had a six-month status report to write, which would have been easier in the privacy of the caseworkers' office, but the milieu staff who usually supervised the boys on campus were even more short-staffed than the social workers. I didn't mind having to fill in. I could sit alone at a small table, pretending to be absorbed in copying information from old reports, while the boys tipped back in their chairs and bounced rubber balls off the cabinets and gossiped

75

and complained. Their speech was coded, and sometimes they looked over at me and dropped their voices, but still, I learned a lot in the common room. If they'd had more places to choose from, they would probably have spent their time somewhere else, where they could speak more freely. But as quickly as the boys discovered new corners to gather in, the staff found and forbade them.

I was supposed to encourage the boys to study, but I didn't. I let them play cards for swiss cake rolls instead. They were thus engaged on that first Friday afternoon when a seventeen-year-old named Joey arrived. I heard Cesar speak up.

"So?" he said.

"Nope," said Joey.

"Why not?"

"It was the old man."

"Damn." A general disappointment in the room, clucking and sighing. "You going to go again?"

"No, man. Are you kidding? Somebody else go."

"Hmm," someone said. I could feel eyes on me. The legs of a chair stuttered across the floor; someone moved a bag so someone else could sit down. I kept writing, the pen scratching quietly.

■ ■ ■ ■

Félix had the spot closest to the window, which was good because he didn't like to be too closed in, but bad because the frame leaked air and it was cold now. In the Indian summer weeks he had boiled, and now he froze. He didn't sleep much anyway since Mrs. Villanueva died. If he was lying there staring up into the dark with that dry feeling in his brain, he would just get up and read. He got books from the library and there was a free bin there too, so sometimes he had books he didn't need to give back. He had taped a sheet of heavy paper around the bottom of the lampshade, which made the light shine downward in a circle no bigger than a dinner plate. As long as he used only that lamp, nobody complained if he was up in the middle of the night. At least, nobody but Carmelo. Carmelo complained about everything. Carmelo was sensitive to the pitch of other people's breathing.

Carmelo was there that night, so: no reading. The boy lay in the dark, with that stiffness in his legs that meant he could keep turning over and over and would never be comfortable. He had a set of thoughts for

77

these occasions, laid specially aside in a mental storeroom. Those thoughts were:

1. What is the perfect meal
2. What is the perfect girl
3. If I had a million dollars

He took number three out and considered it. His memories of the island were beginning to fade, which frightened him. But there were other boys from the Dominican Republic, and one of them talked about it so much that it helped bring some things back. If he had a million dollars, he would live in a mansion in Punta Cana, with a four-car garage. He would walk out the front door, past a fountain like the one Sean Connery had in Los Angeles, and right down to a white-sand beach, which would be full of beautiful girls. He thought of the beach he used to visit with his mother and father; the pink light through a red beach umbrella; a man selling Cokes out of a rucksack, and a jingling sound like change in a pocket. He remembered a yellow dog standing in the surf. Why had the dog lasted so long in his memory? It stood looking out to sea. Columbus landed first in the Dominican Republic. When he had learned that lesson in school he had thought of the beach he knew, with the dog and the man with the rucksack, and white sails just visible, far out at sea. He tried not to think of the white sails now, but once he had started it was hard to stop. They silently appeared on a diffuse horizon. It made a particular feeling happen in his chest, a cold space filled with movement, like the draft through the window. Sometimes the horror of the white sails was that they had always been there.

He went into his memories of the house in San Cristóbal. Sitting and waiting in a cool place, with his face against a banister. Being scolded for wearing no shoes.

If he had a million dollars, one of the cars in the four-car garage would be an Impala. He had discussed the issue with Richard at length, even though it tired him out to speak English for so long, and Richard didn't speak Spanish. Richard said the Impala was the best, because his brother had one and had let him drive it on Long Island, and it was beautiful. What about a Ferrari? Félix had said. Pffft, said Richard. A Ferrari. You spend too much on parts. Félix felt that he shouldn't have suggested a Ferrari to Richard, because it was too obvious. These things were complex and the obvious answer was not always the right thing to say.

The perfect meal was lechón and tostones and rocky road ice cream. Richard may have had a different answer but Félix didn't care what Richard had to say on this subject.

I found Robert Candelario's chart, misfiled with the *F*s, in the annex on the second floor of the administration building. There were no home inspections listed, no relatives to host him on weekends or holidays. He was five feet four inches tall and weighed ninety-six pounds. He had brown eyes and black hair, and a scar across the knuckles of his right hand, indicated with a slash on the outline of a human body that was included in each chart to record distinguishing marks. In the photo his chin was lifted, his shoulders pitched forward, as if he were searching inside the camera for someone he knew. Maybe there was a trace of the little boy in the studio photo there. Maybe I only wanted to see it. I looked for a resemblance to Mr. Ibarra, but couldn't be sure of that either. He was so young.

One of the last notes was written on November 8. *Met with resident in the cottage to discuss his progress in care. Resident stated that he had an alarm clock which was stolen. Resident admitted that the clock was not secured in his locker when he left the cot-*

tage for class on 11/7/67. Resident was reminded to secure personal belongings.

Then, dated 12:00 AM on November 9, 1967: *Resident is AWOL.* Eight hours later, as the morning shift came on, an addendum: *Resident's room was searched. Bag and coat are missing.* On the next page, much creased, there was a missing child report and the name of the officer at the Oakwood Police Department who had taken it.

For an instant I entertained the notion that he'd been kidnapped by allies of the regime. But no: he had taken his bag and coat. Where did the boys go when they ran away? Someone here would know where a boy like Candelario — young, angry about the theft, without relatives to indulge him — would go. This knowledge marked the boys off from adults without diminishing them, and therefore it was precious and would be guarded carefully.

At the Maryland Youth Center, the girls who went AWOL were always said to be with a boyfriend, whether they had been known to have one or not. There was a man in Hampden who, I heard at the time, ran a kind of crash pad for runaways. The girl who told me about it shrugged. "He's all right," she said. "He lets you take whatever you want out of the refrigerator." But another girl who was rumored to have gone there came back with a haunted look.

On a Saturday, Mr. Ibarra left a message with my service saying he wanted to meet me. For an update on the case, he said. He wasn't far away and would be downtown in the afternoon. I was tired from my work week at Saint Jerome and wished I could have stayed at home and reported over the telephone. But it wasn't a good idea to be grudging with clients. I decided to make the most of the trip and take some furniture with me. I had found a good bookshelf on the curb outside a medical practice, dark wood with grooved and beveled edges. I thought it would make my office look more legitimate. I was self-conscious about the worn cushion on the chair and the scarred legs of the desk. I loaded the bookshelf into the back of my car and drove into the city.

I couldn't find parking on the block, so I had a difficult walk to the building, carrying the awkward object in the rain, stopping often to rest my hands and back. Once I arrived, I had only a few minutes to choose a place for it and catch my breath before Mr. Ibarra knocked at the outer door. He came in folding a wet umbrella. He glanced around the office and concluded, with obvious irritation, that there was no stand to put it in. I took it from him and propped it against the radiator. I tried to imagine Philip Marlowe performing such a maneuver for a client and failed.

"Would you like a drink?" I said. "To take the cold off." I had put a bar cart in the corner by the window. Until I could get together the money to fix the leak in my roof, I was filling expensive bottles with cheap whiskey.

"No, thank you. Only the news."

"All right." I sat behind the desk. "There's a boy listed in the records at St. Jerome's who arrived around the right time to be Félix," I said. "But his name isn't the one that was given to the city after Mrs. Villanueva died, and his birthday isn't right. They're close, but not the same." I had taken the photo from the chart room; I would put it back on Monday. I slid it across the desk. "Could this be him?"

His face changed. He rested his fingertips on the paper. I watched his eyes move over it.

"He looks just like his father at that age," he said.

A bubble of happiness rose in my chest. We both sat and looked at the photo. I wished that Mrs. Ibarra could be there too, to see that I had found their boy and was only a few steps behind him. He thought he had no one, but he had these two, who were a line connecting him to his parents.

"You must bring him to us," Mr. Ibarra said.

"He's missing," I said. "This boy, if he's Félix, he ran away from the school in November."

"Missing?"

"He was marked AWOL on the ninth of November. They filed a police report. If you're confident that this is Félix, you and your wife can contact the police in Oakwood and tell them —"

"Are you crazy?" He was shocked. "If this were a matter for the police, we would have gone to them in the first place, not you. This is dangerous. This boy's parents have enemies. Dissidents have disappeared in Puerto Rico, in Spain. You think Balaguer can't reach New York? Every Dominican who works for the New York Police Department came up in the *guardia.*"

"Of course, of course," I said, trying to calm him. "There are ways for us to handle this ourselves. It was only a suggestion."

"I had my doubts about you from the beginning," he said.

I pulled back. On an impulse, I took the photo from the desk and dropped it into a drawer.

"If my services aren't meeting your standards," I said softly, "you're welcome to terminate our agreement and find someone else."

The wind had grown stronger, and now gusts were throwing rain against the window. The cars passing on Fifteenth Street made a rushing sound on the wet pavement. A ringing phone in the travel agency above my office filtered down to us.

"No, of course not," he said finally. "I only need you to understand."

"And I do." I folded my hands, searching for a way back. "What kind of little boy was he, when you knew him?"

Mr. Ibarra relaxed. "Oh, a good Dominican boy," he said, smiling. "An Ibarra. Strong, fast. Playing football with the other children. He was the best player in the neighborhood before they had to send him away. All the other little boys followed him around."

Once, when I was ten years old and taking swimming lessons at the YMCA, I climbed out of the pool too quickly on an empty stomach and almost fainted on the pool deck. I remember my ears ringing from the approaching syncope. Now, in my office, I felt the same pressure and uncanny weightlessness. Under the desk, my feet braced, as if I might have to jump up from my chair. But I kept my voice light. "Ah, an athlete!"

"Oh, yes. And he hated to lose, even then. Like his father. It's a family trait."

"Those things are passed down," I said. "Certainly. From father to son." I was aware of a light going on in the window of an apartment across the alley.

"They are." He nodded slowly, passed his hand over his chin. "I should be going. Please telephone me with any news. Yes?"

"Of course. I'm glad you could identify the picture."

"Mrs. Ibarra will be relieved to know that we are so much closer. But very distressed that he is missing."

"Yes, I wish I had better news."

I gave him his umbrella. He stood and fitted his hat back down over his gray hair, patted the pockets of his coat, gave the umbrella two shakes. I opened the door for him and he pressed my hand. "We only want him back," he said.

After I had closed the door behind him, I went to my desk and removed the sheet of paper with the photo of Félix. I turned it over and read the back for the second time.

Candelario, Robert
Date of birth: 7/22/1953
Next of kin: NONE IDENTIFIED
Allergies: NONE
Medical alerts: HEMOPHILIAC.
EXEMPT FROM PHYS. ED.

I sat for thirty minutes in the empty office after he had gone, my hands flat on the blotter. Then I did a peculiar thing. I called my mother.

She answered on the fourth ring. She liked a hot whiskey and lemon on a cold, damp Saturday afternoon like this one, or she had once, when we had lived together. She would take it in the sunroom, with the paper. Two came to the house. When she picked up the telephone I could hear irritation in her voice at being interrupted, or maybe I imagined it; it was as much a part of her as her accent, which was from the sandy pine flats of north Louisiana and east Texas, or her light rose perfume, a scent I had always thought was too mild for her.

"Kelly residence," she said.

"Hi, Ma."

A pause. "Well, this is a surprise."

I leaned over to the right. If I stretched, I could get hold of the neck of the rye bottle glowing gently in the rainy light. "How are you?" I said.

"I'm fine. Just got back from an association meeting." She was chapter head of the Newswomen's Association of America. "Total chaos, like usual."

Were we chatting? It seemed that we were. I unscrewed the cap and poured a finger into a dusty glass, regretting instantly that I hadn't wiped it out with the hem of my skirt first.

"How are you?" she said.

"I'm all right. Just some — a problem at work."

"Oh!" she said. I was sure that I knew exactly what she was thinking: that finally, after all these aggravating and disappointing years, I had called her with exactly the type of problem that she knew how to solve. She had always been terrific at working. "What kind of problem?"

The rye was practically serrated. I gasped. "They gave me an assignment at the station," I said, feeling it out. "But once I got started on it, it changed."

"Well, that happens."

"I guess it does." The woman in the apartment across the alley was washing dishes.

Her kitchen was warmly lit. I wondered if she could see me, in the dark of the office. Probably not. "I can't trust the boss now, is really what the problem is. The difficulty."

"Ah." She had worked in news for thirty years, and knew all the time that any of her bosses would be happy to cast her aside, given half a chance, and give her desk to someone else. "Well, I can tell you what your problem is, then," she said.

"Yeah?"

"Your problem is that you trusted him in the first place." She laughed.

"Right as usual, Ma," I said. "Well. I'll talk to you later."

"You will?"

"Sure, I will."

"I thought you had forgotten this number."

"You have mine too, Ma."

After I hung up the phone, I didn't like the look of the office anymore. It was too still and too dark. I had smoked a joint with Jane once, and it had infused the ordinary shadows of a familiar room with menace; that was what was happening now. I stood up and put on my coat, and was already outside and halfway down the block before I noticed I had buttoned it up crooked.

CHAPTER 7

I didn't realize how much I was hoping to see Max until I pushed open the heavy door of the Bracken and saw her there behind the bar. She smiled as I came across the room and poured me a drink. Another girl I knew, a waitress from Staten Island who never begrudged a cigarette and was happy to tell the same funny stories as many times as you wanted to hear them, was reading a paperback under a red-shaded lamp on a chain. Everyone called her Peach. There was a dangerous loosening in my throat when I saw them, these two women who knew me a little, at least.

"Thanks, doll," I said to Max, then regretted it, then brazened it out with a smile. She winked.

"Haven't seen you in a million years," said Peach. She tapped the lip of her drink against mine.

"I've been busy."

"So busy you've neglected your drinking?"

"I'm ashamed to admit it."

Max was occupied with other customers, moving back and forth along the length of the bar. The place was beginning to fill up as Saturday afternoon turned into night. I drank slowly, remembering that I would have to drive home, and trying not to think about the cold and dark of the car. I chatted with Peach. As the crowd in the room grew, my face began to flush and my hands itched.

"I'm going to get some air," I said to Peach.

Night had fallen. I let the door swing shut behind me and leaned back against the wall, breathing deeply. The dark gleam of the cars parked along Jones Street was comforting, a reminder of other, happier nights.

I had thought I was doing a good thing with this job. I'd been very stupid. I'd hoped I could do something good and be paid well for it, and now that felt like the ugliest kind of ego and naivete.

Since they were not and could not be his family — since there was no possibility that the hemophiliac son of a wealthy dynasty would be allowed to crash around playing soccer — who were they? I was sure now that the boy was Félix. His birth date, a month and a day off from the real one; and the way Mr. Ibarra had reacted to his photo.

I lit a cigarette and tried to let my mind empty out. Some obvious way forward would come to me if I could only be quiet for a minute.

In an uncurtained window across the street, I saw a man in an undershirt drinking a glass of water. Farther down, a backlit child sat up in bed. I liked how everyone was on top of each other in the Village, the buildings as high as a tall tree and no higher, the apartments on the upper floors close enough that from the street I could make out the figure of a Madonna and child in a lithograph above a stove. In summer, I could hear radios playing through the dense upper branches of the trees. Open windows were such a pleasure.

A police car turned into Jones Street from Bleecker, its lights off. At the same time, a second one nosed around the corner from West Fourth, against one-way traffic on Jones, and stopped. Both doors opened.

If I'd walked away right then, they wouldn't have stopped me. There were lots of people on the sidewalks, and both cars were more than twenty yards away. They probably hadn't seen me standing beside the door of the bar. But I dropped the cigarette and went back inside.

A cluster of boys in eye makeup were laughing and spilling out of a booth, and I had to push through them, knocking into somebody's drink, to get to the bar. Max's back was turned to the room as she made some calculation with her book of receipts. It was too noisy and we had only a few seconds. If I stopped to think, I would run away like any sensible person, and I had made this choice already, to come back inside — I couldn't change course now. I banged on the bar as loud as I could. "Raid!" I shouted. "Raid! Raid! Raid!"

For a split second nothing happened, the hilarity went on, but then a girl to my left took up the cry. The crowd in the room paused, and then heaved and separated, like the Red Sea. I turned and saw Max execute a neat lunge for the jar of tips under the bar, come up stuffing money into her bag, ring the iron bell that hung over the till twice, and throw the list of open tabs into the sink, where it floated for an instant in soapy water and then succumbed. She saw me watching her and beckoned, and I lurched around the bar. Peach had disappeared already, and I wished her luck as we made for the door behind the bar. It opened into a dark hallway. Behind us, I heard the crack of the front door slamming against the wall and the bellowing of police.

"Upstairs," Max said. I could see her white face as she turned. She was holding on to my wrist and I was holding on to hers. She led me up a staircase. "Up?" I said, doubtful. Behind us, I could hear a clamor of voices protesting, chairs turning over. A glass smashed. "Hush," she said. After two flights I saw a knife-thin line of light ahead of us, through which cold air rushed. Max pulled open a door and we spilled out, panting, onto the silver-painted roof.

"The man who owns the building at the end of the block," she whispered, panting, "is a friend of Antonio's. He leaves the roof door unlocked."

The night clouds glowed a dirty orange above us, as if fires were burning somewhere. Sirens raced up Bleecker Street. Voices and hurried footsteps echoed from the alley behind the bar. We ran for the building on the corner, dodging television aerials and clotheslines. The roof door was unlocked, as she had said it would be. We descended into an ordinary apartment stairwell, tiled in a peaky Easter yellow. A child looked curiously out of a doorway as we passed.

"I have a car," I said. I was still bold. The

94

hair that I pushed back out of my face was damp and hot. "Can I drive you somewhere?"

She was ahead of me, and she raised her shoulders in acceptance without turning. "Sure, all right."

"It's parked on Thirteenth Street." Half a flight from the street, I stopped. "Should we wait? Or go out?"

"Go out," she said. "They won't know where we came from. How are you dressed?" She turned my shoulder so she could get a good look at me. "Not like a dyke at all. Like a secretary."

"I had something to do for work," I said, embarrassed. She was in high femme gear herself: false eyelashes, pale lipstick, a glittering swoop of hair above a short orange dress. Cops in the Village, even the vice squad, were blind to femmes. They arrested butches in droves.

The child we had passed appeared one flight up, peering down at us through the railing. "How did you spot them?" Max said.

"I was having a cigarette outside and I saw them coming. Both directions at once."

"It's been a long time. I thought they had gotten bored with us," Max said.

"Somebody must be up for reelection."

We pushed out together onto the noisy

95

sidewalk. I looked over my shoulder toward the Bracken, just once: lights bounced and streaked across the facades of Jones Street. A paddy wagon was backed up with the doors open, and in the spot where I'd been smoking I saw a crowd of women, their hair falling over their faces, their arms bent behind their backs. A bolt of guilt at having made it out. We turned the corner onto Bleecker, Max fastening her coat as we walked. The night felt colder. Would it rain again? There was something unstable in the humid air. I was aware of Max's hot presence at my elbow as we walked north through the Village. I began to wonder what exactly I was doing.

I waved ceremoniously at the car when we found it. "Ta-da." I got in first and leaned across to open her side. I was short of breath, still nervy from our escape. Few things felt as good as not being arrested. Her hair brushed the roof; she tucked the flaring edge of her coat in beside her and pulled the door shut. The seats were vinyl, cracked, and cold.

"Where are we going?" she said.

"I was going to ask you the same thing. Aren't I driving you home?"

"I guess so," she said, sounding disappointed. "It's the Aurora on West Sixty-

96

Second." But then she sat up. "No," she said. "Let's not. I want to go someplace fun."

I turned pink and was glad she couldn't see it. The lift of a night not ending yet. "Another bar? We could go uptown."

She laughed. "God, no. I mean real fun. The beach? A mountain? I wouldn't mind seeing a mountain right about now."

I noticed that I was gripping the steering wheel as if we were in traffic already. She made me so nervous. She wanted a mountain? "How about the Catskills?" I said.

"I would," she said. "I'm not joking."

"I'm not either. There's a road atlas in the glove compartment." I turned out into Thirteenth Street. We would go up the West Side and into the Hudson Valley, and it could take all night, I didn't care. We would find a hotel somewhere. The word *hotel* slunk around in my brain. Max took the road atlas out and turned the pages, tilting it toward the windows so she could catch the glow of the streetlights as we passed through Chelsea and merged onto the West Side Elevated Highway. My car protested on the on-ramp and vibrated until I could ease it into fifth gear. The black of the Palisades rose up across the river, crenellated with the lit apartment blocks of Union

97

City. A legion of billboards to our right advised us to stop for gas, for drinks, for a show.

"You don't have somewhere to be tomorrow?" I said.

She laughed. "You mean at work?"

"I guess not."

"No, they'll make him fight to get the liquor license back for a day or two."

"Anybody expecting you home?"

"My roommate." So the Aurora was a boarding house. "But not expecting me, really. She won't be sitting up in a chair. What about you?"

"I live alone." And yet I thought of Jane, huddled on my stoop. She told me once, the first spring that we were together — the only spring we were together — that when I left her alone in my house for a day while I went to work, she searched my bedroom and the second-floor office for a journal, a diary, something. But there wasn't anything. She told it like it was a funny story — the woman who kept no diary. As if everyone kept a diary! As if the chief drama of that story were not, in fact, her searching my house! I'd been angry when she told me, but I'd also been astounded by the thought of a person wanting so badly to know me.

Jane had found some photos from Argentina once, in the sideboard in the living room. Tourist snaps I had taken on quiet days. A man selling peanuts out of a cart in front of the immense fortress of the Teatro Colón. Students on the steps of the Facultad. A photo I had asked an acquaintance to take of me, in sunglasses, under a date palm in Parque Centenario. "What were you doing there?" Jane said. "I was a student of languages," I said.

Max and I drove in silence, while the Bronx presented itself on cascades of granite to our right. "Where are you from, Max?" I said finally.

"Los Angeles," she said.

"Oh? Why did you leave?"

She didn't say anything and I thought I had offended her. "It's just that everybody makes it sound like heaven," I said. I put my hand on the gearshift unnecessarily, and then moved it unnecessarily to the emergency brake. Then she said, "I came east for college and I stayed."

"College?"

"Vassar. What about you?"

"No college," I said.

"No, I meant where are you from?"

"Washington, DC."

She was quiet again. Then she said, "I

can't think of a single thing to say about that."

I shouted out a laugh. "You could say, 'Cherry blossoms.' Or, 'The Smithsonian.' "

"Oh, yes, cherry blossoms."

"They're very beautiful," I said.

"I'm so glad to hear it."

"If you're going to give me a hard time, you'll have to pay for tolls."

"Lucky thing I have so many nickels," she said.

We passed over Spuyten Duyvil, the river letting in beneath the highway just as the far bank of the Hudson towered and pressed close, and crept on through the remains of the Bronx into Yonkers and out into Westchester County. A mountain had been her idea, but it was me and my car that made it real, and being in charge of this venture weighed on me. Max sat so lightly in the passenger seat, checking the pages of the atlas as we went, looking out through the passenger window with her chin on her fist — waiting for whatever it was, this plan I had scooped us into.

"Are you hungry?" I said.

"God, yes. I would have sent somebody out to get me a burger just about now if we hadn't been raided."

The lights of a town showed at the foot of

a dark ridge. It was nearly eleven o'clock and I doubted we could get a hot meal, but if there was a gas station nearby they might have something. One of those menacing piles of sandwiches wrapped in plastic. I turned off the highway and we bumped over the seams and cracks of a smaller road, down to an intersection where a red light blinked for the benefit of no one but us.

"There's a Sunoco," I said.

I filled the tank. Max stayed in the car. It was colder outside the city, and I wished I had a scarf. The wind carried the river with it. I paid inside at the register, counting the money in my wallet: it might be enough for a single meal and one night in a motel, but not more. I wondered how much Max had and how I could possibly ask. I remembered the payment I got from Mr. Ibarra and felt, again, as trapped and doomed as I had in the office. Under the eyes of the ancient and papery attendant at the counter, I perused the two short aisles of candies and crackers, trying to guess what Max would like. I chose a bag of peanuts and two packets of crackers filled with yellow cheese. Mr. Ibarra leaving my office and going — where? Not back to some floor-through Fifth Avenue apartment, as I had imagined before. Some barely furnished base of operations? A hotel room? A Balaguer safe house in New Jersey or Queens?

When I got back to the car, Max had turned the dome light on and was reading a paperback, holding it up close to her face. I walked around to my side, watching her in the bell jar of light. The night around us had drawn very close. At the edge of the parking lot, scrubby woods screened off a village block of small, pale homes. The low cloud cover of the day had thinned, and the moon rose in a long strip of space. I rarely got to see the sky black. In the city it was always washed with color. Max's shadowed face, still with concentration, caused a soft pulse of fear in my gut. An errant sensation from the dark woods. It was only that I was afraid I would make some mistake, ruin whatever this was supposed to be, which I was supposed to know. Fail to stay here forever, which was what I wanted, since what waited for me in the city was another mess, another set of choices that all made me either a dupe or a hack or a harder person than I really wanted to be anymore.

I settled in next to her. She smiled at me. The book was *The Power and the Glory.*

"Crackers," I said, handing them to her. "Peanuts?"

"I'm starving." She took them happily

from my hands. "You know what? The girls talked about a place up this way when we were at Vassar. One of those summer places with a hundred rooms. For the winter they had a sauna and some things like that. There was a lake."

"In Poughkeepsie?"

"Near it. It was called Oskar's."

"All right," I said. "Let's go." In my role again, the bold squire. I kind of liked to be led around myself, but I always went for this type of girl, and that's not what they did. It was one of the inconveniences of my personality.

"I don't remember where it was, really," she said.

"We can ask someone when we get close."

Poughkeepsie, with its high bridge, was nearly another hour up the road. By the time we reached it I was beginning to feel more comfortable. Max handled the radio and made conversation. She knew half the Village. I mentioned a gallery show that had just gone up, and it turned out that Max knew the painter, had been to some party of his at a beach house on Long Island, had surprised him in a pantry with a Vanderbilt. She gossiped with pleasure but no malice. Since I couldn't keep up with her, I grew quiet, although I liked the way she talked.

Everything was a story. At a gas station where I could look out from the car and down the stairstep terraces of streets and wood-frame houses to the river below, Max jumped out and asked the counter man for directions to Oskar's, and got back in with a map of Dutchess County and the route traced in pencil, as well as a pamphlet for the place itself. Swimming pools, tennis, boating, it said. What would be left for us? A bar would be nice, I thought. We were close to Vassar now, and Max tapped on the glass as we passed fields where she had camped during freshman rush, a church where she had sung Reformation music with a choir, an ice cream shop where she had worked two summers. "Don't let me go on and on," she said finally. We were turning up a narrow road by then into total darkness, no houses anymore and no lights.

"It sounds like you were happy here," I said.

"Very happy," she said. "I even had girl-friends."

"They allow that sort of thing at Vassar?"

"They would have some job on their hands if they didn't." She laughed. "I had a boyfriend at first, actually. They would throw mixers for us — for the Vassar girls and the boys from Rensselaer and Bard. We were supposed to get fiancés and I did, for a little while. I was still deathly afraid of myself then. His name was William. I went into a hysterical fit halfway through my sophomore year and mailed him back his ring. Poor thing. I wonder where he is now."

I thought to myself that in another life, if things had gone differently for me at seventeen, this might have been my story too. It was what girls from my neighborhood did. Girls from families like mine, from schools like mine. We drove in silence while I thought about it, and then I said it out loud.

"If I hadn't messed up so badly in my junior year of high school," I said, "I probably would have gone to a place like that. That's what my mother wanted."

"The mystery speaks," Max said.

"I'm not a mystery," I said.

"Ha! The other girls at the bar talk about you. Always swanning in by yourself. Dressed the way you are. Somebody asked if you were married. They thought you were an adulteress with money."

"Dressed how?" I said. Then: "An adulteress?"

"I disagreed. I said no way you were married. Money, yes."

"But my clothes aren't —"

"I know they're not, but I know how rich

girls dress, too. A certain kind of rich girl. They don't go to Bergdorf and buy up the season. They get a crepe de chine from the consignment room at Eula's."

I smiled. I was embarrassed. Sometimes you think you're doing something unexpected, or that you can't be read at a distance. "I was brought up that way."

"Ah, no," she said. "I've made too much noise and now you've run away." She looked out the window, at the dark, undifferentiated woods. "I'm sorry, I'm being rude."

"No, you're not." I was thinking of the Silver Spring Cotillion, still the banner event of the year when I was a girl. The limousines parked in the circular drive of the Corsair. The golf club, where my father wouldn't let us go even on guest days, because the pool was segregated and he was a member of the Civil Rights League of Greater Washington.

Haloed lights appeared through the trees, then a white-painted sign: OSKAR'S RESORT HOTEL. An oar, looped with rope, was arranged along the top of the board. We proceeded down a paved driveway and into a lot. The place was rusticated and gigantic, with half-timbered gables upon half-timbered gables unfolding in both directions to the edge of the woods. I could sense cold water in the dark: the lake at the back of the hotel. I was starting to be concerned about the money in my wallet, but there were only a few other cars in the wide lot, and I hoped for off-season rates. When we pushed through the doors, the scale of it knocked me back: the lobby was furnished with acres of vinyl sectional sofas that repeated in shifted formats until they reached a grand staircase ascending to a mezzanine floor. A general impression of brown and gold soaked into me. Max was already chatting with a night manager, an elderly woman with very black hair seated at a desk the size of a fishing boat. "I've got cash," Max was saying. I intervened gallantly, offering a check. She hesitated, then let me pay. This financial operation made me blush. I had missed the part of the conversation where the room had been described. How many beds? I couldn't imagine she would have asked for only one. We went up in an unattended elevator to the third floor and walked an endless, silent hallway. "Look at this," Max said, pushing open the door to our room. "A view! I think she liked me! A closet case for sure."

Two beds. "It's big," I said.

She bounced in the chairs, opened the drawers in the night tables. "No Bible," she said. "You think they put them away for the off-season?" She went into the bathroom but left the door open, and I heard running water. "It's good and hot," she said. "God, I feel filthy."

"Are you hungry?" I called.

"Starving. Do you think the kitchen is open?"

"No, no." It was one o'clock in the morning. "But maybe they have something." The bathroom door closed and I heard water rush in the pipes. I called down to the lobby and was told they could send up two chicken sandwiches, the price of which made me blanch. But I was too hungry to sleep, so I reconciled myself to it. The sandwiches arrived a few minutes later in the hands of an aged bellboy, and I was relieved to find that I still had enough cash for the tip. I ate my sandwich standing up at the window, though with the lights on I couldn't see the view that had delighted Max unless I cupped my hands around my eyes. A spread of unbroken woods and a bit of the end of the lake. Jane would have known all about this kind of place. Hadn't she worked a few summers in a hotel in the Finger Lakes? Many of her teenage stories included the words *summer people.* She had saved a little boy from drowning once in

Seneca Lake, the child of a Montreal family down for the season. I heard the bathroom door open behind me.

"I'm a new woman," Max said happily.

I missed her; it was awful. I turned around, and Max was there, bent over the room service cart with its solitary sandwich, her hair loose and wet, her skin pink, wrapped in a white bathrobe with the hotel stitched in miniature over the left breast.

CHAPTER 8

Félix was sick of Paulie, who was supposed to split the tips with the busboys and the dishwashers but kept some back. Paulie thought nobody knew it because he did the counting at the concierge stand in front, but he didn't notice that Félix could see him from his post cleaning the glass front doors.

The restaurant was an Italian place that cost a lot. Some days Félix worked from opening at eleven o'clock in the morning until after closing at ten o'clock at night, running plates and clearing tables. He was slower than some, because he checked over and over for steak knives and broken glass in the bins. He had tried to explain it once to a cook who was watching him unload dirty dishes, but he didn't have the word for it in English, and when he tried to describe the problem, the cook looked at him like he was crazy. "Too much blood if I get cut," he

110

said several times, and then gave up. He had dim, awful memories of a week in the hospital and a blood transfusion when he was six, after he stepped on a nail in a field on the hacienda.

It was a hard job. The minute he sat down at the end of his shift and took off his shoes, his feet would begin to pulse with heat, and he sometimes felt static-shock crackles of pain in the joints of his toes. He wore tennis shoes. Dennis, the head cook, said those were the wrong kind of shoes for this kind of work, but they were all Félix had. Maybe he could buy different shoes next month. At least he had plenty to eat. Plates of fettuccine Alfredo with the cooks before the dinner service, and then shrimp scampi at end of shift if the moods were right. Sometimes he was allowed to bring cartons of noodles back to the house, if they were going to throw them away.

The house had a big turret and a little one and wooden shingles falling off the front, like a sea monster rotting away. A week and a half's pay, every month, went to Ruth, the landlady, who came to collect it in person. Another boy at Saint Jerome had told Félix about the house, in what already felt like another life. The downstairs smelled like mildew and it was always cold. Most of the boys slept upstairs, in the three largest bedrooms. They had come from various places and most didn't like to be asked about it. The older boys crowded into the bedroom in the back, where the windows were newer and fit tight in the frames, and the kerosene heater they kept could make some difference against the cold. The younger boys and more recent arrivals were left with the front rooms, where the wind whistled through the gaps around the frames, never letting you forget it. Félix hated the cold but there was one consolation. From those front rooms there were big views, clouded though they were by the dirt on the glass, of the town sloping down to the river. On bright days the river was sometimes dark; on dark days it could shine. Ships passed, dull black or red, separating the waters. The bridges were high to let them under. A river reminded you that every place connects to every other place. An idea that was sometimes too much to bear.

When Félix was falling asleep, he sometimes had dreams that left him breathless, more exhausted than afraid. He was trying to build or locate something with cheap tools, bad directions, poor eyesight, the wrong language, ears stuffed with cotton.

Mrs. Villanueva, who was his family but wasn't his family, who was a friend of his mother who never appeared, was bending over him and speaking Spanish in her soft voice. There were his mother and father who had said they would send for him in a little while. It had been almost three years. When Mrs. Villanueva was alive, they had sent him letters without return addresses, letters that didn't use his name. They never said when they were coming. He didn't understand what they wanted him to do. How long he should wait.

This grinding mystery hovered close. He batted it away in the mornings; he ignored it as it pressed around him on his dark walks home. At Saint Jerome he had a textbook in which a few passages of a translated *Don Quixote* alternated with photographs of the original pages, dated 1605, and he was overcome by a sense of recognition and dread. This was the problem: his language mutilated, faded with age, missing parts of words, familiar orders inverted, blotted with *x*'s where other letters belonged, irretrievable.

"Washington," Max said, sitting on her bed as I sat on mine. "So. What does your father do? Any brothers or sisters?"

"No brothers and no sisters."

"And your father?"

"He died. My mother's an editor at a magazine." At the bars and parties where I went, when I could be bothered to go to bars and parties, we didn't ask each other about our families. A rule that I had learned without noticing it before now. Too many of us had cut ties with them or disappeared, or were trying to disappear.

"I'm sorry," Max said.

I nodded.

"What do you do, anyway?" Max said. "You're a teacher?"

"I'm a caseworker at Saint Jerome," I said.

"Ah," she said. "Those poor kids."

"Yes," I said, and then we ground into a silence. I got up and went to the bathroom, washed my face, and stood looking into the mirror, wishing I had a toothbrush. I had brought myself here, to this ridiculous pass, with this girl who was too pretty and who had come along thinking that I could make something exciting happen, or some vindication of our night, the chaos at the bar, and I couldn't. I was disappointing her. My reflection came in and out of focus. I was tired. My hair was puffed up from the rain. I tried to smooth it with my hands, which didn't work. Then Max was there in the doorway, her arms crossed over her chest.

"Have I done something wrong?" she said coolly.

"You?"

"Yes, me. Have I done something wrong? Because you're very quiet." She uncrossed her arms, then crossed them again. "Maybe you have a girlfriend? You could have said."

Had I not been talking enough? She had so much more to say than I did. "No, I don't have a girlfriend."

There was a little heat in her eyes. "What, then?"

I stared at her, speechless.

"There was no need to drive me around if you didn't want," she said, shrugging. "I'll go home in the morning."

"Max, no," I said, reaching out with both hands, then not sure what to do with them. "You haven't done anything. It's my fault."

"Why did you bring me up here?"

I dropped my hands. "Because I couldn't leave you there," I said. "Because I wanted to get away. Max. Look at you." Her wet hair tendrilled across her neck, and her eyes were bright. She had washed off her work-day makeup in the bath and I could see her freckles now. I took hold of the sash around her waist and pulled her closer. "Please forget everything," I said. I kissed her; she leaned into me. Her hands were hot and damp through my dress.

It was tentative at the beginning, normal enough for a first time, and then for a while we could laugh in the dark and take our time. Finally, a rush and a shock. The room had grown stuffy and hot. I climbed out of bed, making some joke, and opened the window a few inches. The night was still and cold. I smoked a cigarette in the draft, and when I lay down again, she was already asleep. I lay awake for a while, thinking pleasant thoughts, and then less pleasant ones.

I woke at four thirty in the morning from a nightmare, with the sensation of having pulled myself bodily to consciousness from under deep water. I had been dreaming that a face was at the window. The curtains were open and the moon lit a corner of the rug. Max was breathing so quietly next to me that I leaned closer to hear her, as if she might have stopped. I felt alone and pursued, and fought the urge to wake her up. The room had gotten cold. I got out of bed and closed the window.

In the dry-mouthed aftermath of our night, a hangover forming, self-consciousness returning, my anxieties crowded in. I remembered a story I'd read in the *Times* a few years before: in 1956 Trujillo had a man killed who was in exile in New York, a dissident named Galíndez who was getting a PhD at Columbia. Galíndez was kidnapped by Dominican agents in New York and flown back to the island and murdered for the offense of writing a thesis. A Dominican nurse who had also been on the flight was later found with all her bones broken in a burnt-out car at the bottom of a ravine, a detail from the article that had stayed with me, because the nurse's friends said she couldn't drive.

Balaguer had been Trujillo's right hand and had succeeded him after he was assassinated. When I read through the Latin American pages in the paper on Sundays it was clear that Balaguer ran the island in much the same way Trujillo had. He enjoyed the support of the United States, in American dollars — just as Trujillo had, until shortly before the end. There were more Dominicans coming into New York now than there had been under Trujillo, because Balaguer's violent repression had reached such a peak that no one was safe on the island. The prisons were still full. Farmers still found bodies in the cane fields. Balaguer held parades. He flew new American-made airplanes in formation across the skies of Santo Domingo.

I didn't know what Balaguer's people could want with this boy, but I couldn't let them find him before I did. The boy was alone, and I was responsible for him in some way, now that I knew about him. That was something — I held onto it. The idea that someone depended on me, even if he didn't know who I was.

The safest thing to do with the counterfeit Mr. Ibarra was to keep playing along. I needed the money anyway.

In the morning Max said, "Well." Looking down at me, propped on her elbows. Smiling in a way that made her seem impossibly far away, but benevolent, like an empress.

We got up and I put on a bathrobe; she didn't bother. She came out of the bathroom chatting, combing out her hair, which made me blush. She kept up her light talk until we were in the car, and then she said, "I have some old haunts to visit."

I was about to turn the key in the ignition. "Oh?"

"Yes, I'm going to stay for a bit in Poughkeepsie and then take the train back. If you don't mind dropping me in town."

Once again the feeling washed over me

that I had ruined everything, ruined a chance that I hadn't taken seriously until it was directly in front of me. "Yes, of course." '

We drove back down the wooded road, which was stripped of its mystery in the daytime: a leafless understory filled with brambles in a forest of insubstantial young trees. This ground had been cleared once. The day was neither cloudy nor fine. Max was quiet, not chattering like before.

"Do you miss California?" I said after a while.

"I do sometimes," she said. "You wouldn't believe how beautiful it is."

We entered Poughkeepsie proper and made our way through tidy streets. A troop of women in heels and netted hats spilled down the stairs of a domed church. Max sat with her fingers across her mouth. "You know what I miss?" she said. "I play the piano. I thought about going to a conservatory. I can't have a piano here. But I play sometimes in a church." She tapped the glass. "You can drop me here."

I stopped at the curb and Max fixed her hair, checked to make sure nothing had spilled out of her bag onto the floor, straightened her jacket. Her hair was soft now, since she had washed it in the hotel, a light honey brown. She looked younger than she did in the bar. Just a girl, really. I felt ordinary, obtuse, a large machine poorly calibrated. I searched for something to say. Max turned and I blurted out that I would like her number.

"All right, but give me yours too," she said.

She produced a notebook and a pen, and ripped a page in half. We exchanged numbers, and then she was abruptly out of the car and walking away down the sidewalk, settling the strap of her purse on her shoulder.

■ ■ ■ ■

II
JANUARY 1968

NEW YORK

■ ■ ■ ■

Where did they go at night? I had been watching the logs, not only in my cottage but in the others, when I could find a reason to look at them, or when no one was around. The New Year had ticked past and we had settled into an icy January. The logs were brought each afternoon to the casework office to be reviewed by the supervisor, and I paged through them then. On Friday nights, and on Wednesday nights, a few late returns. I read back through a few months, looking for patterns. Michael and Cesar, always together, were late once every third week; they'd spend the following two weeks serving out their restrictions and be free again in time for the cycle to repeat itself. Some boys were AWOL for whole weekends, but usually those boys' workers knew where they had been. "His grandma's place," they would say if I noticed the absence aloud. "He's not allowed to go there because she

123

won't let me do a home inspection but he goes anyway." Or: "With his girl, probably." Or: "His brother just came back from upstate; I knew I wouldn't see him until Monday." The late returns didn't have the same quick answers. During a quiet lunch hour, I cross-checked the cottages. There were six other boys that clustered on the late returns on the same nights as Michael and Cesar.

The way to get a person to tell you something when he doesn't want to is to know something about him, and offer not to tell. The Monday after Poughkeepsie, I told Mrs. Allen that I was going to need a few hours one morning for a doctor's appointment, and volunteered, with profuse apologies, to cover an evening to make up for it, taking one of the many empty milieu spots. I asked for a Friday evening, a shift that no one wanted to work. Mrs. Allen readily agreed.

On Tuesday night I was exhausted. It had been a long day. I'd been ready to leave at five and had been surprised with an intake, a skinny boy just arrived from Staten Island, holding a grocery bag filled with clothes, an expression on his face that I recognized now — hostility that was a substitute for fear.

He was fourteen and a half. He refused to answer my questions at first, and when I asked him what he'd had for lunch he couldn't tell me. I walked with him to the cafeteria, let myself in with the staff key, and made him a bologna sandwich. We sat together in the dining room, which was lit only by the kitchen lights at the far end — Mr. Chambers liked us to be discreet when we used the kitchen after hours, because if we weren't, it would bring the boys out of the common rooms and cottages, like moths to a flame. The boy ate the sandwich quickly and silently. I made him a second one and brought a chocolate milk from the bin in the refrigerator. He relaxed enough to look tired, and answered the questions I had left. It was six thirty before the boy was settled in Cottage 6 and I could clock out.

At home I switched on the television and the radio. I liked a little commotion in the evenings. I poured myself a whiskey and made a thick sandwich of my own out of the meatloaf I had made on Sunday evening. *The Girl from U.N.C.L.E.* was on the television. An old man was supplying Stefanie Powers with a clip-on earring that could mist a room with knockout gas. She had the kind of hair I had desperately envied when I was seventeen: shining, auburn, mysteriously inflated from within.

I was afraid to call Max, but I also knew that I had to. It had been two days now since I left her in Poughkeepsie. I put the sandwich aside to stare into the molding around the edges of my parlor ceiling. I had hoped that she would call me and spare me this. But she had not.

I dialed the number she had given me and listened to it ring. At four rings I gave up hope, but relief and disappointment kept me on the line for another three. It was her room in the boardinghouse; of course she wouldn't be at home at this time of the evening, she would be at work. I hung up and washed all the dishes in the kitchen, cleared the counter, swept the floor, considered mopping it, stopped myself. I found the number of the Bracken in the Manhattan telephone directory in the hall. There, too, the phone rang and rang. She had said it would take time for the owner to extricate his liquor license from the grip of the city. All that tension and effort, dissipated into nothing. I went back to the television. Now it was *The Fugitive.*

She had said she was staying in Poughkeepsie. Maybe she was still there.

For an instant I pictured her sitting in her boardinghouse room, watching the telephone ring, cutting eyes at her roommate.

Dr. Kimble escaping again from the wrecked train. Running through a desiccated California wood. The radio in the kitchen was switching to jazz. It seemed very difficult and complicated to get myself to bed.

St. Jerome's was quiet on Friday evening, because all the boys in good standing who had family to visit had gone home. The boys who were left gathered in the common room or sat up playing cards in the cottages, or lingered in the cafeteria and dining room, which were kept open two extra hours. There was ice cream, and a television on a cart was wheeled into the common room: small compensations for the boys who had to stay. Milieu staff walked the hallways and grounds in shifts, running flashlights over the hurricane fences, stopping at the equipment sheds and garages to check and double-check the locks. A quiet, restless feeling prevailed. The boys were subdued, and would have picked fights with each other if there had been more opportunity to do so.

Mr. Jenkins didn't approve of women walking the grounds alone at night, but neither did he want to waste another staff member by having me babysat, so he gave me a flashlight, irritated. It was a sharp, cold evening in late January. I had dressed warmly, in sturdy shoes. I went first through the dormitory, where the youngest, newest boys and the ones who needed the closest watch were assigned to sleep. Only a few doors were open: boys reading comics or magazines, arguing over a radio with a wisp of an antenna, lying still and looking at the ceiling. Those ones I stopped to question. "You feeling okay?"

"Yes, miss."

I remembered evenings like that, although I had so few of them compared to the residents here. My term at the Maryland Youth Center had been outside of time — an eternal hum of lights, shifting inside a uniform that was too tight under the arms, other girls whispering through the walls: it had lasted forever, but for only a month. Some of these boys had been at St. Jerome's for three years. I had written letters on my long evenings at MYC, then torn them up. There was no thought I had had while I was in juvenile detention that I could safely share with a living soul. I had filled dozens of pages and every last one had ended up in the bin outside my room, or down the incinerator chute set in the wall by the staff station. Each time I returned to my room I began again. This time I'll get it, I thought. I'll say it a different way. I wrote letters to my best friend Joanne that were too ardent. I lay for hours trying to imagine how to begin a letter to my mother, who had put me there. Something that said both *You're all I have* and *You're nothing to me.* She wrote me once, asking if I needed a warmer coat. I never answered. I did need a warmer coat.

The yellow silence of the dormitory was oppressive. I was relieved to step back outside into the brisk dark and begin the circuit that Mr. Jenkins had described for me. Around the perimeter of the campus, behind the cottages, looping once around the school, and making a lengthy dogleg to cover the playing fields, the baseball diamond, and abbreviated soccer pitch that edged into the woods on the north side. A fat moon was rising above the trees, whitening the frost on the grass. I saw a lit cigarette floating in the shadows behind a maintenance shed, but caught no one but the groundskeeper, whose name I hadn't learned yet.

"What do they have you doing this for?" he said.

"They're short-staffed. I don't mind it."

129

He shook his head sympathetically. "Ridiculous."

I kept going, keeping away from the tree line. I had noticed paths at the edge of the woods in daylight, and wondered if the boys used them, and if they did, whether they had the nerve to do it at night. These were almost all boys from the city: they would be unsettled by the comprehensive darkness of this hill. I was a little unsettled by it myself, separated now by so many years from the old trees and private yards of Chevy Chase. I was used to Brooklyn, where the streetlights shone so brightly into my sitting room that I could have read the paper by them if I left the curtains open.

I had checked the logs. Michael and Cesar and three of the boys who followed them everywhere had signed out with the rest who had off-campus privileges to go to Oakwood after dinner. They were allotted two hours, and were expected back by 8:00 PM, but Michael and Cesar often came straggling in at 8:30 or 8:45, not quite late enough to raise an alarm but late enough to be docked points. The walk from the campus to Oakwood proper took fifteen minutes on the main road, which led in a long curve down the hill past the guard station and along a row of white- and gray-colonials

130

whose residents wrote regular letters to the editor of the *Oakwood Journal* to complain about the Saint Jerome boys. They were accused of vandalism, theft of garden tools and supplies, casting menacing looks, making peculiar noises in the dark. On an investigative lunch break, I had learned that there was a faster way to travel: you could get from the delicatessen in Oakwood back to the center of St. Jerome's campus in eight and a half minutes via a steep dirt path straight up the side of the hill. In daylight it was pleasantly secret and overgrown; at night, it would be a close tunnel of whipping branches, with the black woods pressing in all around.

As curfew approached, I headed toward the southwest side of the campus. I was beginning to feel the cold, although I had been walking fast. I smoked a cigarette and wished I had brought a thermos of tea. It was 7:50 by my watch. I hesitated near the garage where the school vans and the groundskeeper's truck were parked, and switched my flashlight off. Behind me, from the road and the main gate, I heard young male voices. They carried clearly in cold, dry weather like this. It would be the main group, coming back from their off-campus jaunt, full of meatball sandwiches and doughnuts, buzzing with new intrigues. I walked in a circle, trying to keep my blood moving. After a few minutes, the portico of the main dormitory building, where check-in was done before the older boys could disperse to their cottages for the night, went quiet behind me. The stars had grown brighter.

A bubble of laughter in the woods, and then the sound of branches breaking underfoot. I moved into the shadow of an overgrown holly. A voice — Cesar? I held still. A shape appeared at the end of the path and I switched my flashlight on.

"Noo," he said quietly. It was Michael, shading his eyes from the glare. Two other boys stopped abruptly behind him. "Shit," someone said.

"My goodness," I said.

"Who's that?"

"It's Miss Davies."

"Who?"

"Where have you all been?" I said.

I saw a look cross Michael's face — anger, which was gone almost as soon as it appeared, as if he couldn't find a use for it. "We had passes, miss," he said.

"You're late."

"We're sorry, miss," Cesar said, in a singsong so subtle in its irony that I couldn't

132

respond to it.

"Who's here?" I pointed the flashlight at the other boys, who hung back. Two boys from Cottage 6, which was Gladys's cottage, and one more I didn't recognize. "You know something?" I said. "I have a feeling about you five. I'm not sure you do go to Oakwood."

They shifted on their feet. Cesar was looking up curiously into the trees, as if trying to identify their species.

"No one ever seems to see you there," I improvised.

"Miss, we were in Oakwood," Michael said. "We went to the movies."

"What did you see?"

The Jungle Book.

"You went to see a cartoon?"

"That's all they're showing, miss."

"It was pretty good," Cesar said pleasantly.

"You boys can go check in," I said. "Michael, stay here."

He sucked his teeth. As the other boys filed past, defeated, I caught a smell like the syrup in a jar of cherries.

Michael and I stood and watched them trudge away up the lawn.

"You weren't in Oakwood," I said. "You were up on the cliffs."

I felt him tense up without looking at him.

133

"No, miss."

I said nothing. The silence was an advantage to me. I felt around in my pocket for another cigarette and lit it. They would have found some damp clearing to drink sweet liquor in. I had heard the milieu staff talk about walking up to the cliffs on night rounds to be sure there were no boys up there. The cliffs were just to the south of Oakwood; it was a short walk to a wild piece of land. It had once been part of the parcel that the utopians had settled. At the edge, Chambers had told me, there was a forty-foot drop straight down to the river. "It's a cold night to be sitting in the woods," I said.

My eyes had adjusted to the dark without the flashlight. Michael looked steadily at the grassy slope leading up to the school. He was trying to decide if it was worth denying.

"I don't know what you're talking about, miss," he said.

"You shouldn't be taking the younger boys out there. They look up to you."

He kept his face turned away. He didn't seem drunk. His feet were planted and he didn't wobble, but there was sugar and liquor in the air. He was moderate, for a sixteen-year-old. I was sure I had come in late to Barrington in much worse condition more than once. Something came back to me down the years: the face of the night matron, looking at me furiously under the white light of the guard cottage while I stood there trying not to be sick. She had said awful things to me.

"I don't take anybody anywhere," he said.

"Don't lie to me," I said. "Every time I see trouble, you're in the middle of it. What about that boy Candelario, who ran away? You were a friend of his."

He was startled. "No, miss."

"What happened to him?"

Michael squinted. "You work for the bureau, miss?"

I let him think it. "Where'd he go?"

"I don't know."

"Give me your best guess."

He was chewing his lip.

"Do you worry about him?" I said. "Some people wouldn't. But I think you do. Because he left and never came back. Most of them come back."

"Not all of them."

"I think Catholic Family Services is lucky the word didn't get out." I dropped my cigarette. "If you don't have anything to say, that's fine. I'll go and find Mr. Chambers and let him know what you've been doing."

An awful equilibrium between us, in the

dark. He looked me full in the face and I saw myself changing before his eyes, from an ordinary intractable grownup to something less, a person willing to scheme and negotiate with a child. There was something in my throat.

He shook his head. "He was upset because somebody took his clock. He had brought it from home."

"All right."

"And then he was gone. He left."

"So where did he go?"

"I already said I don't know."

"Where do boys go when they run away?"

"I don't know."

"You've spent a lot of time here," I said. "You know what goes on."

He looked at me, a little of his self-possession coming back. "Yeah, I do."

"All right. So where?"

"I don't know. He didn't have people."

"Where do boys go, then, when they don't have people?"

"They work."

"Work where?"

He shrugged. "Somebody said a restaurant."

"A restaurant?"

"After he left. Somebody said Bobby was talking about going to work in a restaurant."

136

"Where?"

"I don't know, miss. That's just what I heard somebody say."

I could feel that I had reached the end of it, what he knew or what he would say. "All right," I said. "You can go."

CHAPTER 10

At home that night I made tea, turned on a
lamp in the parlor, drifted around trying to
think up an appetite. The house still needed
furniture. I had been filling it slowly, piece
by piece, but it had been a year already since
I bought it and it still felt bare in places. I
wondered where my grandmother's furniture had gone. My family seemed so small
sometimes, a scrap, my mother and me only
tenuously connected to the aunts and uncles
and cousins who had spread out across the
sandy flats of the Gulf Coast, up through
the Midwest, and into the mountainous
silences of the Dakotas and Montana and
Idaho. A family that had landed in this
country from its various old-world disasters
and had been maintaining its moody quiet
ever since. New calamities were consigned
to silence as quickly as they happened —
lost homesteads of which no photographs
survived, great-uncles who disappeared into

western jails, a grandfather who killed himself during a hard winter somewhere in Montana, his own personal end of the world in a place I couldn't have picked out on a map. Was there ever a family that was less interested in remembering itself? My father's mother had been an exception, a small, talkative woman who kept her hair covered. She was Armenian, and she had fled the Adana massacres in 1909 to be a prairie bride. She died when I was seven and I had only a few memories of her. When she came to visit, my father would install her in the best chair and she would catch one of my hands in both of hers and talk to me endlessly in a trill of English blithely mixed with Armenian, her eyes kind and intent, apparently confident that I could understand her. I caught bits of what seemed to be fond and funny memories, churches and schoolyards and goats and chickens that floated, syntactically isolated, around our carpeted Chevy Chase front room. I think now that she was the only one who escaped her village, so she carried her memories alone and was engaged constantly in the project of impressing them on the minds of others. She was like the runner at ancient Marathon, exhausting her life in the effort to deliver a message. A little neighbor boy stealing eggs, a church decorated with flowers for a feast day. An orchard that belonged to the family. I don't remember much. I was so young when I knew her, and my father is gone.

These thoughts pursued me upstairs, into the dark second-floor hallway. I stopped in the doorway of the second bedroom that I had turned into an office, which Jane had appropriated for a few weekends of work when the construction in the lot behind her own apartment had been too much for her to bear. She had left behind a bed jacket that she liked to write in; it was hung over the back of the chair. I recoiled from the sight of it and went back downstairs.

Without giving myself too much time to think about it, I dialed Max's number again. She picked up on the second ring and I carefully tipped myself over a cliff.

"Hello, it's Vera," I said. "I'd like to see you tomorrow."

There was the briefest pause and then she said, "Well hello, stranger."

"I tried you earlier in the week . . ."

"Oh, I was still —"

"Upstate?"

"Yes."

Now we were nowhere in particular. I tried to decide whether I should repeat my invitation.

"Tomorrow I'm afraid I'm busy," she said.

"Oh, yes, sorry, I know it's very late to make — I know it's — I just thought that I would. That I would say hello —"

"Sunday morning I'm playing piano at Greenwich Church on Eleventh Street," she said. "Would you like to come?"

"To church?"

"Yes, to church. For musical reasons only. It's a beautiful church, with a little green lawn."

"Well, all right. Yes. I would."

"Wonderful. It's the ten o'clock service."

"I'll see you there."

Sunday morning was sunny and cold, with one of those high blue skies that looked like it might crack, and faint cirrus streaks at the foot of Sixth Avenue. I had come with a hat pinned over my hair and my thickest scarf. I was at risk of looking foolish. I had worried overnight that this was a test that I was failing — that any self-respecting bar pickup would refuse to appear on a Sunday morning for a chaste hour of Brahms and choral music. That this might be the date she fobbed off on the girls she kept in some second tier. I felt anxious and unkind. It was her impulsive goodbye in Poughkeepsie

141

that still stung. I paused in the back of the nave, conducting an inventory: my shoes were clean, my hat straight, my hair reasonable. My mother had taken me to a Methodist church in Arlington on a handful of Sundays a thousand years ago. I remembered cutting shepherds and sheep out of colored paper in a basement room, and my mother's brisk reemergence after the service, looking as if some part of her architecture had been braced while she was gone. She never spoke about her religion, and some time after my father died, she went back to spending Sundays on the sunporch, reading alone. I found a gold cross in her jewelry box once and she said only that it had been her mother's.

The church was beautiful: the sun lit a Tiffany angel bestriding a blue earth in a window above the altar. The wooden beams overhead were painted red; the plaster of the sanctuary ceiling was blue. The pews at the front were full. I chose a place at the back and looked up into the brass light fixtures.

Max appeared a few minutes before ten, stepping out of the rectory in heels and a dark skirt, and took her seat at the piano. I watched her pause, her wrists cocked, eyes down, before she began to play. The chatter

142

in the pews fell away. I didn't recognize the piece. It was bright and sweet, and she was smiling to herself. I watched her shift and reach, bringing her attention down lightly and firmly on each figure. It was so intricate; she moved so quickly. The pastor had entered, unnoticed, and stood in the pulpit. Max came to the end of the piece and let her hands drop into her lap.

The sermon was about the erosion of the family. Lately there was always a low chatter of disapproval in the city, in newspapers and magazines, in gatherings of adults. Its subject was the hippies: loose-haired teenagers clustered under trees in Tompkins Square Park in the rain, issuing plumes of smoke into the branches, and girls in beads sunning themselves for stupefied hours in the Sheep Meadow. The summer before, this anxious hum had reached a pitch that put it on the evening news, and cameras panned across Golden Gate Park and down the sidewalks of San Francisco. I had seen some of it, the sunlit faces just vague white spots on the screen of my struggling television. Some girls danced slowly alone, revolving in circles, and bare-chested young men with beards loomed suddenly into the camera's eye, beaming and offering handfuls of something — bread? It had happened so fast, an alien civilization that sprang from the earth. They all seemed to know what they were doing, as if following a script. *Life* magazine said that young people from good families were abandoning their homes and streaming westward. It was the phrase *good families* that made me realize that many of the hippies were from places like I was, from Chevy Chase and Bethesda and Grosse Pointe and Westchester and Lake Forest. I tried to imagine this countercultural wave crashing on the shore of B-CC, my old high school. We still hadn't dared to wear blue jeans when I was a student. Our stockings were subjected to tests of transparency. The pastor was speaking on the prodigal son, the way that parents should welcome back their wayward children when they returned. This was not a fire-and-brimstone kind of church, and he was restraining himself from the commentary on brassieres and similar topics that usually dominated.

I wondered how queer it all was: I couldn't quite get a handle on it. All these long-haired, lovely young men in gaudy clothes, and yet the breathless speculations about hippie sexual practices that I heard were all confidently heterosexual. The groupings that I saw downtown tended toward young women arranged happily around a young man, like a frame around a painting. And they went out to California and lived in flophouses and ended up with babies. What would I have thought of it, if I were seventeen now? What did Max think of it? She sat at her piano bench, her back to the keys, watching the sermon as if it were her own private show. I would have liked it then, probably. I would have wanted to run away. Any circus would have done.

At the end of the sermon, after Max played the recessional hymn, I threaded my way out of the pew and stood in the side aisle, under a window in which Jesus waited beside the still waters. Something came back to me, also in stained glass: the windows of the Catholic church where I had gone to Mass once or twice with Joanne after spending Saturday nights at her house, when we were still kids and nothing had yet gone wrong. Those windows had shown the thirteen stations of the cross circling the sanctuary. Jesus had been racked and pale, his forehead bloodied. Mary wept. Was something lost, in all the gentleness of a church like this one on Eleventh Street? Wasn't Calvary more present in the world than the green meadows and still waters? They had shown a napalmed forest in Vietnam on the evening news three nights before. Or was the napalm here, too, implied in the face of the pacific angel over the altar? What drives people into a sanctuary but fear and violence?

Max was approaching, but being waylaid every few steps by parishioners who clasped her hands. She looked happy.

"Hello," I said when she reached me at last. "That was beautiful."

"You liked it?" she said. She squeezed my elbow and we kissed on the cheek. "Is it just you?" she said, glancing around.

"Just me? Yes, just me." Should I have brought friends?

"Are you starving? I like to get some eggs at the coffee shop around the corner on Sundays."

Hope surged. We went out into the cold. The coffee shop was tiny, a row of seats at a chrome counter and a few two-person booths in the steamed-up window.

"Where'd you learn to play like that?" I said, after we had ordered and the waitress had brought the food to our booth. I had toast with black coffee and Max had a breakfast spread out before her that looked like it had been taken from a Rockwell painting.

"Oh, you know — I took lessons for years and years. I had very good teachers."

146

"They must have been," I said.

"My parents thought I was a prodigy. I wasn't a prodigy, but they were happy to spend money on lessons. It was lucky that I loved to play so much. I was a kind of showpiece."

"A showpiece?" I said.

"Well, you know — sons in a family like mine — sons are one thing. Daughters are another. It was a nice talent to have. It kept me busy. The women in my family tended to have trouble staying busy."

"It sounds dynastic. What are you, an Astor?"

She looked levelly at me, her expression pleasant but serious, and then said, "No, I'm a Comstock."

"Oh," I said, and then again, more slowly, "Oh." I thought of the Comstock Collection, a converted army barracks near San Diego filled with Romantic paintings. Then I remembered that the Comstock Institute of Texas was where my mother's father had trained as a petroleum engineer. "Of Comstock Oil & Gas."

"The very same."

Something in her tranquil expression wobbled. She turned her attention to the street, where a silent ambulance had stopped in front of an old folks' home across

the way, its lights flashing. So the bartend-
ing job was — what? A lark, maybe. An af-
fectation to liven up her youth.

As if hearing my thoughts, she said, "They
cut me off. I was an idiot." A little shrug.

"What happened?" I said, although I
could guess.

"After the college fiancé, they had another
boy they wanted me to marry. He was a —
I could tell you the name of his family but
it probably wouldn't mean anything to you,
and I hate talking that way. I didn't want to
marry him and they fought and screamed,
and then I ran away for a week with my girl
— we went up to Santa Barbara. My parents
had one of their private security men follow
me and he caught us together."

"He caught you?"

"He'd been a Pinkerton, I think. He was
creeping around the windows of our bunga-
low at night. When I got back to Los Angeles
they told me they knew everything and I
had to marry this boy or be disinherited. So
I was disinherited. I was twenty-two."

I finally put down the cold toast in my
hand. It plinked on the plate. I tried to
square all this — the rending of ties, the
gothic glitter — with the winking girl behind
the bar. "Why did you say you were an
idiot?"

"Ah, well. Because that girl left me. Because if I had held on another three years I would have had a trust, which I don't think they could have taken away without a lawsuit, which would have meant their lesbian daughter in the papers, which they never would have allowed. Youth — you know."

"So you have nothing?" I said.

"Not a thin dime."

"Do you speak to them?"

She laughed. "If Episcopalians sat shiva, they would have sat shiva for me." Her voice was light, but her body had gone tense. I had been brought up in a prosperous suburb full of diplomats and lawyers and women who took tennis lessons, but this was something different. I thought of Hearst Castle at San Simeon, which I had seen in a photo essay in *Life* magazine. It was a sprawling mansion on a hill. Zebras, which had amused some child once, and then multiplied into herds and gone native, grazed alongside Hereford cattle on the slopes. There were carved and painted ceilings, looted from the churches of Europe after the First World War, with char and smoke still visible on them.

"So what did you do?" I said.

"I moved in with my girl for a few months

and got a job in a restaurant. I had no idea what I was doing, but she helped me. And then when that fell apart, I packed up my things and came back east. I came on a bus and I had just enough saved from working in LA for a week in a boardinghouse. I got that job in the Bracken on the sixth day. I've been here four years."

"I had no idea I was in such lofty company," I said.

She glanced at me, measuring, and then her face went tight. Maybe she thought I was making fun of her. She leaned back from the table, smiling now, all charm. "Well, what do you do with your Sundays?" she said.

I tried to think of an answer that might extend this moment in the damp heat of the restaurant, let it clarify itself, but she seemed to be preparing to go, and the fact was that I had work to do that day. "I have to drive up to Saint Jerome," I said. "A weekend shift."

"All work and no play," Max said. "Well, it was nice of you to come."

She asked for the check and with some sleight of hand I got it away from her. She seemed to like that.

"Again, yes?" I said.

"Sure thing," she said. She drowned a

150

little more sugar in the last of her coffee and emptied the cup. "You know my number."

I drove up to Oakwood in my rattling car, wishing I couldn't feel the drafts so keenly around the windows. The day felt colder the longer it went on, the sun barely free of the trees on the ridges. I reviewed the information I had. The night Bobby Candelario left St. Jerome's was a Thursday, and on Thursdays only one bus left Oakwood. It was the Valley Flyer and it made local stops for twenty miles, covering the inland towns that the train didn't reach and then coming back down to the river at Peekskill. He wouldn't have dared to take the train — it would be full of staff, going both directions. How long would a fourteen-year-old boy have to stay on a bus before he felt that he was far enough away from a place he never wanted to see again? How long could he stay on a bus before he was too hungry to go any farther? The Thursday bus stopped at White Plains, Valhalla, Thornwood, Pleasantville, Chappaqua, Millwood, Crompond, Peekskill. I stood in the bus depot in Oakwood, where four concrete berths for coaches exhaled cold air and gasoline into a small waiting area. The schedules had schematic

151

maps printed on the backs that I distrusted. I had my own, an AAA foldout in my purse. Three little girls huddled around their mother on a hard bench like a pew, dolefully eating cookies. It was a quiet place. I asked the ticket man if he'd seen a boy like Bobby a couple of months back, identifying myself as a worker from up the hill. He said he'd only been hired in December. There was no one else in uniform in the depot. I bought a ride on the next Valley Flyer, which left the depot in two hours. It made the same stops on a Sunday as it did on a Thursday as far as Peekskill, after which it went express up to Poughkeepsie, an extremity it would not have reached on the evening Bobby left. I had a sandwich at a café across the street and came back at two o'clock. The 2:15 was already idling in the berth. I sat on a bench with an open book, thinking about Félix. Had he waited long? Maybe he had planned his escape ahead of time and knew the schedule already, so he could slip down the hill just before the 8:30 bus rumbled to life. Someone had done an inventory of his effects after he had gone, which I found in his chart. His bag and winter coat gone — it was cold in November, especially cold along the river — and both pairs of trousers. His dress shoes remaining, his tennis shoes gone. No socks or underwear left in the dresser. It was a church in White Plains that provided the winter coats. I had seen the request forms. The boys didn't like them and called them "church coats." Some had their own winter jackets, worn proudly back to campus after visits to family. But Bobby had probably had a church coat. They were all the same color, a dark green.

The boys were given a dollar in spending money every week. The bus ticket cost seventy-five cents. Maybe he had saved for a few weeks before he left, or maybe he had run away with twenty-five cents in his pocket. That was more likely, since it looked like it was an impulse, the distress of the stolen clock, that made him go. He was young enough to make that kind of decision.

I took a seat close to the back of the bus. I wasn't sure what I was looking for. I wanted to think like him, try to feel where he would have gone. A place that looked warm and alive from the road. A place not too far and not too close. He had lived a long time in Sheepshead Bay. I wondered if he liked to be near the water. He would have remembered the blue of the Caribbean. It made me sad to think of a child used to white

153

sand beaches and a warm salt wind landing in the far reaches of a Brooklyn winter. And then to be brought to a place like this. Bare woods slid by. Sodden lawns, a mail truck making a slow circuit of a subdivision, white siding against an off-white sky. The remains of old snow, packed and sculpted by rain, lay in blackened ridges along the curbs. The bus turned onto the highway.

An old woman across the aisle from me was singing softly to herself in Spanish. She had crochet needles, and something white and pink was growing stitch by stitch between her hands. "Regresando," she sang. "Regresa-a-a-ando." A song I had heard once from a Puerto Rican singer in a club uptown. Puerto Ricans in New York spoke of the island the way the Jews in Babylon spoke of Israel. In my last boardinghouse, I had been friends with a girl from Ponce who had come up for art school, an illustrator who did evening and weekend work for an advertising firm in Midtown. I heard her sometimes crying on the telephone to her mother in the great room downstairs, and she would come up afterward with a distant look, her eyes very black and her cheeks pink, as if she'd been communing with spirits. She had postcards of Ponce tacked up all around the mirror in her room; she went home three times a year, and she used to tell me I could stay with her grandmother if I ever came to visit the island. I had never gone, but sometimes I would sit in her room drinking Nescafé on winter Sunday mornings, looking at those photographs, those endless confrontations with a gentle sea.

Where were Bobby's parents? No — correcting myself. Félix's parents, Dionisio and Altagracia Ibarra. If they were in prison in the Dominican Republic, as the false señor and señora had said, then I didn't have much hope. I had read stories. People didn't really come back from Trujillo's prisons, even if they left alive; the same was true of Balaguer. They were the same prisons, the same guards. It didn't bear thinking about. Where would this boy go if I found him? If his parents were unreachable, his wealthy relatives a fiction, what would I do with him once he was rescued? I looked out the window at the highway, the gray fog of the woods. A farm appearing in a space between two Levittowns, a few cows on a slope; forlorn, as if they had washed up there. If he had no family, then he would stay in foster care. Knowing the truth about his parents wouldn't make any real difference. He would gain nothing except the knowledge that he was in danger and his parents were lost and in pain.

I was going about this all wrong and in the wrong order. I was impatient with myself for not seeing it sooner. Maybe his parents were not in prison at all. I had no reason to think I had been told the truth about them. They might be anywhere, and I needed to find them, too.

The bus advanced from town to town, rumbling down off-ramps into Pleasantville, Chappaqua, Millwood, Crompond, pausing briefly in front of town halls and department stores. I noted the places where a restaurant that would appeal to a fourteen-year-old boy with less than five dollars in his pocket was visible from the bus stop — Pleasantville and Peekskill, with a Shakey's and a Howard Johnson's, respectively. I wrote down how long it had taken to get there, what towns we had passed on the way, which stops let more people on and which let more off.

If the parents were in prison, after all, then what would Balaguer want with the son? If the family had already been defeated, why pursue the boy here? If there was no hope, why go so far to snuff it out?

At Peekskill the bus waited for thirty minutes before setting out on the return journey, and I got down and found a telephone booth. I could still remember the number. I had never written it down. An indifferent female voice answered on the third ring.

"Anne Patterson calling," I said. "Is Gerald Carey available?"

CHAPTER 11

I chose our meeting place. Not the coffee shop he liked on East Fifty-Second Street but instead a dark bar in Hell's Kitchen whose collection of tiki accents — woven palm fronds, hula girl figurines, strings of dusty silk hibiscus — failed to conceal its Irish-cop nature. I picked it because there were booths in the back and they never played music before ten o'clock. Maybe I also picked it because he would dislike it. He was fastidious. He liked things bright and clean; there was an essential, almost aggressive wholesomeness to him. I arrived first and saw him come in, edging through the street door as if he preferred not to touch it. He spotted me, but his expression didn't change. It had been a year.

"Hello, Gerry," I said.

He dropped his hat on the table, and then slid into the booth across from me and laid one large hand across the other.

158

"Vera," he said. "To what do I owe the pleasure?"

"I got you a drink," I said. I pushed an old-fashioned across the table with the tip of my finger.

He looked into it without touching it. "I didn't think you ever wanted to speak to me again."

"I didn't," I said. "But I got into something."

I watched his face. When I first met him, I had thought he was oblivious, because he didn't seem to react to what he was told, to adjust to small adjustments in other people. Later I realized that he grasped everything, and that his languor was strategic. He nodded toward the bar and said, "I can't drink alone in company."

"I don't need anything," I said.

"It's been a long time, Vera. To our health."

He rose and went to the bar, and returned with another old-fashioned. We clicked them together. I took a cigarette from my pack, and he lit it. He had a heavy gold watch I hadn't seen before. Maybe he'd been promoted. The green-shaded lamp over the table buzzed, and the place seemed very quiet.

"You didn't come after me when I left," I

said. "That's something, at least."

He shrugged. "You had completed your assignment."

I had. I had gotten myself out of Buenos Aires after the coup had closed the ports, after my contact had turned on me and run, after spending three months holed up with a man I'd met from Texas in an apartment on Calle Tucumán, waiting for a break. Calling Gerry every day from pay phones all over the Centro, holding on to a hope, long after it stopped being sensible, that he would conjure me an exit visa. Every day I had expected the police to knock on the door. In the end I had made my own exit, leaving the Argentine sovereign territory on a fishing boat, under a false name, concussed, dehydrated, and sick from the subpolar atmosphere of the Strait of Magellan.

"What is it?" he said.

I drew the ashtray across the table. "A missing Dominican boy."

"Are you freelancing?"

"Yes."

He looked disapproving. "You have no backing."

"I didn't have much backing with the CIA either."

He looked away.

160

"An old couple came to me and said they were looking for their great-nephew. They said his parents were in one of Balaguer's prisons and he was here in New York. But when I looked into it I could see that they weren't who they said they were. They're not his family."

"Who are they?"

"They must be Balaguer's people. I don't know what they want with the boy, but if he's who they said he is, his parents are in trouble with the Dominican government. I need to know where they are."

"You think the people who hired you are Dominican agents."

"Who else could they be?"

"You need to get out of this, Vera."

"How, Gerry?"

"Pull up stakes. Disappear. Go out of state for a couple of months."

"It'll be dangerous for me if they know their cover is blown."

"Is that it? You could come up with something if you really wanted to."

I avoided his eyes.

"So why don't you?" he said.

"Why don't I what?"

"Get out of it."

I flinched. It was uncomfortable to have my impulses probed like this. And it seemed

161

so obvious anyway. Why make me say it?

"Because he's just a kid. He has nobody."

He let that stew. Then he said, "So what's your plan?"

"It's developing."

"All right, Vera."

"I'm looking for him; I've had some leads. But I need to know where his parents are."

"What if they're in prison, like they told you?"

"Maybe he has other family."

"How are you going to get the agents off your back? Even if you find him and you find his parents?"

"That's the part that's developing."

He set his fingertips against his temples and closed his eyes.

"You're alone in this," he said.

I waited for him to go on.

"Why did you ask me here?" he said.

"I need help."

"Vera."

"You must have people in the Dominican Republic," I said.

"Of course I do. Because Balaguer is friendly, Vera."

"Friendly to who, exactly?" I said.

"To the United States. You know that."

"He's hardly any better than Trujillo."

"Trujillo was friendly too."

"He was a psychopath."

Gerry spread his hands, as if to say: Who are you talking to? To what audience?

"Where are your people?" I said. "The embassy?"

"Please, Vera."

"I need to know if the parents got a visa. Their names are Dionisio and Altagracia Ibarra."

"Please, it's a small country," he said. "They wouldn't have left under their real name. There are still informants everywhere. A third of the island is reporting on the other two-thirds. Or maybe the other way around."

"I need to know if they're in prison like I was told," I said.

He shook his head. He extricated his own cigarettes from his jacket pocket and made a lengthy process out of lighting one. Something in him was withdrawing. "They don't share that information with us."

"Don't they?" I leaned closer. "That's all their own business?"

He said nothing. His hair was neatly combed; he wore a suit. How was it possible that in only the space of a year, he had begun to look displaced in time? He wasn't so old. I would have been surprised if he was more than thirty-five. I was only twenty-seven myself, and I felt it too. There was something jangling and chaotic happening out there that we were not a part of. Who were we?

"You're asking too much," he said.

I touched his hand. The anger was back, surprising me, heating my face. "You owe me this much," I said.

The music clicked on. *I go out walking, after midnight, out in the moonlight, just like we used to do.*

"I have a man I can ask who has a man he can ask," he said finally.

Three days later my service had a message from him. I was due at Saint Jerome for an afternoon shift in a few hours, but I went out for a walk and I called him back from a telephone booth at the edge of Grand Army Plaza.

"They're not in prison," he said.

"You're sure?" I practically went up on tiptoe.

"Almost sure. Almost is the best I can do. You know how these things are. They're an important family."

"Yes."

"So the important families, if they go to prison, there are records. They go on a list."

"All right. So where are they, if they're

164

not on a list?"

"Evaporated, I guess."

"So they're gone? Gone where?"

"I don't know any more than what I've said already," he said.

The trees creaked in the wind blowing up Flatbush Avenue. "Thanks, Gerry."

"Yes, well." He sighed. "You're welcome."

I hung up, hesitated, and then called my service. The girl came on the line, sounding tired. "You have a message from a Mr. Ibarra," she drawled. "He's asking for a return call. Shall I connect you?"

"No, not right now." There was an idea forming, and it made me feel nauseous and hot, like looking down into deep water. I hung up the telephone and began an argument with myself.

How else can you do it?

But you don't have to do it at all.

I crossed to the library, a place where I had gone many times to unspool my confusion. It took itself so seriously, with its gold-leaf figures of Whitman and Moby Dick in the facade, its fifty-foot lobby, that it made me take myself more seriously, which discouraged my usual evasions and self-deceptions. I went into the fiction room on the right and sat at a table with my head in my hands. There was no reason in the world not to tell Mr. Ibarra that I had failed, withdraw from the case, and go back to trailing unfaithful wives on their Saturday shopping trips around Queens.

And yet the thought of doing that made me furious. It was an adolescent kind of rage, my throat closing. Félix was a person — I kept thinking — who was alone. A child who was alone, as I had been. Whatever Gerry thought, whatever Jane might have thought if she knew about this, it was unbearable to drop it now, when a path had already begun to open that could bring me to his parents. Because it had occurred to me that there are public records everywhere, and one thing that's always public is a marriage license, and a marriage license lists an address.

It would take a lot of money to get there. But I could keep cashing Mr. Ibarra's checks. I went back out to Grand Army Plaza and called the service back.

"A return message for Mr. Ibarra," I said. "Are you ready?"

"Ready, miss."

"Some progress. Working on a lead in Pennsylvania."

She read it back to me.

"That's it," I said. I would tell them I had caught a rumor about some niece or nephew

166

of Mrs. Villanueva in Scranton or some-place, and had gone to investigate. I needed a cover for leaving town. I walked back toward Eastern Parkway, navigating the plaza's ring of traffic, looping past the histrionic Neptune with his trident. I was beginning to be afraid of the undertow in all this. I walked along the fine western margin of Prospect Park, where sandstone mansions with many-lobed windows looked over the elms and plane trees and broad lawns. The sky felt close on this side of the park, now that the leaves were gone. I could almost see how to land it all. It could be done. I turned into the park, to walk the wooded path that led to Lincoln Road. I would have to go to Santo Domingo, find the old estate, talk to whoever was there.

The neighbor woman had had enough. There had been a man parked for a long time on Webb Street. The sun had set and night was falling. Down a block or two, at the end of Avenue X, seagulls roosted, as docile as chickens, in the riggings of sail-boats. The lights were coming on in parlors.

The man was smoking. The window was down, although it was a cold night and get-ting colder. He had been there for nearly an hour. Moving slowly, his movements hard to discern through the reflection of the sky in the windshield, which was still a little pink. It was his cuff that showed he was smoking, a muted white drifting up to the face and disappearing again.

The car was a Chrysler Newport — tan, with new tires. It didn't look out of place on the block, which was lined with single-family homes and duplexes warding off the oceanic atmosphere with vinyl siding, modest vehicles parked along the curbs.

When the street was truly dark, and the lone streetlight at the far corner had come on, the man climbed out of the car and walked toward the late Mrs. Villanueva's house. He passed the front-porch steps without pausing and stepped over the low ornamental fence and into the side yard where her clothesline still hung. He was lost to view around the back of the empty house.

The neighbor woman decided that it was time to intervene. She didn't like people creeping around and she doubted he had a good reason to be there. She stepped back from her window and pulled on her overshoes and coat, picking up the flashlight she kept by the door for good measure, because it was heavy and she wasn't afraid to swing it. She reached the sidewalk just as the man came back around the side of the house.

She fell back without meaning to. He was tall, his face shadowed by a hat, his shoulders bulked by a thick scarf. He barely seemed to have seen her. She blocked his path.

"Go on and get out of here," she said, "whatever you're up to."

He stepped around her. She faltered.

"I've seen you here before," she called after him. "A while back. I remember your car."

He didn't turn. She watched him go, gripping the flashlight, wondering if it was still worth calling the police. He got back into his car.

"I've seen you before," she called after him again, but he had rolled the window up, and the sound of the car starting shook the quiet of the street. There was an exhalation of blue exhaust, and then he was gone.

I packed quickly, remembering the last time, when I had prepared to go to Argentina. Nerves made me irritable about little things, unable to find my sunglasses, fluttering in a panic for ten minutes over the Anne Patterson passport, which turned out to be in a book where I had left it. It was not like Argentina, I reminded myself. For Argentina I had had no return ticket. I hadn't known how long I would be gone.

This time I had a round-trip ticket, purchased that afternoon at a travel agent on Jay Street. I had given myself a week. I didn't have any vacation days yet at Saint Jerome, so I was forced to give my notice. I was ashamed of myself, in a funny way, as if I really were a caseworker. I told Mrs. Allen over the phone, making up a sick mother to allay my guilt, and listened to her voice go cold. I tried not to think of the boys in my cottage. I couldn't have meant anything to them yet, anyway.

I hesitated over a swimsuit. This was not a vacation, and yet, how would it look not to have one? Gerry used to say that an agent should prepare like an actor. Curious, and friendly with a few young actors during those first years in New York, I had read Stanislavski's book *An Actor Prepares.* I liked it, the way the director harassed the acting students with koan-like instructions, how the students behaved when they imagined an audience and how they behaved when they imagined they were alone. Maybe I envied them their effortless conviction of the importance of what they were doing. I had never felt that anything I did could be both pleasurable and important. That was probably my mother's influence. Her only

170

leisure was reading the newspaper and playing tennis at the club, and even that she did with her colleagues and their wives, and played to win.

But I had learned something about concentration from Stanislavski's book. Choose a point of attention, he said: the Nearest Object. I had used this when traveling with a false passport. In the customs line, I would choose a little thing, a child's hat, a red suitcase, and focus on it. It helped me stay calm. Stanislavski had steered me right before. If I was a woman on a Caribbean vacation, I should pack a swimsuit. When I was finished, when everything else was ready, I took a .22 pistol down out of a box in the attic, unloaded it, and zipped it into a camera case at the bottom of the bag.

■ ■ ■ ■

III
JANUARY 1968

DOMINICAN REPUBLIC

■ ■ ■ ■

CHAPTER 12

The French doors to the balcony were open and sunlight came through a fabric awning, tinted blue and yellow in stripes. The hotel was modest, concrete, painted pink, but it managed five stories and I was on the fifth, privy to a slice of a view past the casino billboard across the street: a glittering tropical sea, the horizon attended by small white clouds so still they appeared to have been painted there. I had fallen asleep as soon as I checked in; my flight from New York had been early. The breeze was warm, coming from the beach and picking up the smell of frying meat as it passed over the few blocks that separated my hotel from the grander ones along Playa de Güibia. I was hungry and thirsty, but a strange, light feeling clung to me. No one knew where I was, and it was warm here. My street in Brooklyn was iron gray, and there had been ice on the trees when I stepped out to wait for my cab that morning, evidence of a late freezing rain. On the rattan bedside table I found a can of Canada Dry that I had had the foresight to buy from a café in the Santo Domingo airport, and went to the balcony to drink it, then came back to call down to the desk and ask for a continental breakfast to be sent up. Traffic was noisy on the street five floors below, and music drifted up from sources I couldn't see. At the end of the block there was a small park, a few benches in a circle admiring a statue of a man in a frock coat, who was orating with one hand spread over his heart. I would see later that it was Duarte, father of the Dominican nation. While I drank the ginger ale I watched a man with a cart flay young coconuts, one after another, with balletic strokes of a machete. A row of tiny children in uniform came out of a school and were led away down the street.

The casino billboard was a photograph of a showgirl in a towering headdress with tiers of radiating feathers like an Aztec god. She wore a lamé bikini and cascades of fine chains, and her expression was uncertain. Room service arrived, a woman in a yellow uniform who brought a tray out to where I was sitting and told me, while I searched through the pockets of my discarded jacket for the pesos I had already converted, that dollars were fine. I passed her one and she backed out.

The showgirl and I confronted each other again while I ate the buns glazed with sugar and drank the strong coffee. She looked like she couldn't understand what I was doing there, but was trying to be polite about it. I wondered for the tenth time what Gerry would have said if I had told him my plan. "You have no backing," probably. I lit a cigarette.

Before I left New York, I had had some business cards made up identifying me as the assistant to a location scout in Hollywood. Sometimes a flashy story got you further than an ordinary one. I thought about how I should put my shoes on and choose my lightest dress for this day that was getting hotter and hotter, and go downstairs.

But I stayed in the plastic chair on the balcony, and when I finished my cigarette I lit another one, with fingers that were beginning to be unsteady. I had a raspy cough from smoking too much.

I had passed under a sign that spanned the street as I came from the airport that morning: SANTO DOMINGO DE GUZMÁN, OLDEST CITY IN THE

AMERICAS. The sea was an impossible color. I had read that Dominicans believed there was a curse on Columbus's name, and refused to speak or write it. Hotels named for him burned, airplanes crashed, and newly ordained members of the Order of Christopher Columbus died of strokes and heart attacks one after another, like dominoes falling. The Arawak dead did not forget. I felt a doomy lack of equilibrium. Balaguer admired the man and liked to talk about him, although even he, out of an abundance of caution, called him only "the Admiral."

I had liked stories about sailors and explorers when I was in school, and it was mostly for the way they paired the misery on board the ship — the filth, the exotic grimness of words like *hardtack,* the barrels of fresh water dwindling in the hold — with visions of islands like this. The wretched Spanish or English fleet always came at last, when all seemed lost and the men were on the brink of mutiny, to a white shore lined with palms. The air was always heavy with flowers. Native people paddled out in longboats, offering fruit and roasted fish. And then the story that I liked most as a bloody-minded eleven-year-old, the reversal of these themes, or maybe the real point of

178

them: Magellan and his starving crew landing on a Filipino beach and being cut to pieces by the army of Lapu Lapu, the king of Mactan. Magellan had wanted to convert the king to Christianity. My sixth-grade textbook, with beautiful reserve, said that Lapu Lapu "refused this overture." He also declined to return the body. When I first read that story I was taking riding lessons with a daughter of a Filipino diplomat, and she told me that people in Cebu and Mactan still saw Magellan's ghost. "What does he do?" I said, breathless. "He rolls around on the beach and yells," she said, laughing.

I put on a short dress and dug up my largest sunglasses from the bottom of my bag. My legs were pale. The New York summer was a long time ago now.

In the lobby I picked my way through a few fellow tourists standing next to islands of luggage and found the directory I was looking for at the end of the broad reception desk, sheltered under the leaves of a banana tree in a pot. "It's very safe here," I heard the bellhop saying to a tanned pair of grandparents with Miami tags on their suitcases. "The police are very hard." There it was, the *Palacio Municipal,* City Hall. I wrote down the address and gave the young girl at the desk five centavos for a map of the city. The bellhop was telling the old couple where they could gamble. Through the glass doors at the back of the lobby, a turquoise swimming pool rippled in the noon sun. I went the other way and stepped out into the glare of the street.

Motorbikes rattled past. A taxi discharging a passenger in front of a hair salon was blocking a convertible trying to make the turn at the end of the block, and the second driver was half out of the vehicle, one leg in the street, preparing to air his grievances. A honking city bus vibrated and fumed behind them. The street was lined with concrete multistory buildings, their facades complicated by balconies and strung with wires and cables. Expensive handbags gleamed in a vitrine across the street, each arranged on its own plinth, like a Greek urn. I saw my chance and ran toward the taxi, which was still idling in the street as the grand lady who had stepped out of it laboriously counted the coins in her purse. "Where you going, miss?" the driver called out.

"City Hall," I said.

"You getting married, miss? Where's the groom?"

I was out of practice and Dominican Spanish was fast, the consonants eroded. It took me a second to catch up with his joke.

"I guess I lost him," I said. The woman finally paid, and I dropped into the back seat and pulled the door shut. The cab inched through traffic. I was glad to have dark glasses; we were surrounded on all sides by bright windshields, shining chrome, sprays of water lit brilliantly by the sun as shopkeepers and doormen showered the sidewalks with hoses.

"I picked a busy time," I said to the driver.

"It's always a busy time."

After twenty minutes the street opened into a broad plaza, paved with white stones, where a colonnaded municipal fortress stared down a few palms and a dry fountain. I paid the driver and stepped out. It was approaching one o'clock, and men in dark suits, their jackets slung over their arms, walked in pairs and smoked under the palms. The entrance was an immense set of wooden doors that bulged with rivets and looked like they could repel a battering ram. They were propped open, and I stepped into the dim, marble hush with relief. At the far end of the lobby were four narrow, grated windows, lit with weak yellow lamps. A row of clerks waited there in varying states of collapse, observing my approach as if I were an enemy vessel they had sighted from the shore.

ARCHIVOS said the sign over the third window from the left. I tacked in that direction.

"I'm looking for marriage records," I said in Spanish.

"Marriage records," he repeated.

"Yes. Public records. The records of marriage licenses."

"For what purpose?"

"It's a family matter." Bigamy, I thought. Maybe someone's been bigamized. Or questions of illegitimacy have been cast on a birth. It could be lots of things. The clerk got down from his stool and made a production of turning around to consult the large clock on the wall behind him.

"It's twelve thirty," he observed.

"Yes?"

"The archives are closed from twelve thirty until three o'clock."

I sighed. "They open again at three?"

He was irritated, as if that didn't follow. "Not on Tuesdays."

"So the archives do *not* open again at three?"

"The marriage records are not open to the public in the afternoon on Tuesdays."

"But the rest of the archives are?"

"Yes, but not the marriage records."

I took a deep breath and set my hands on

the counter beneath his window. "Would I be correct to understand that the marriage records will be open to the public again on Wednesday?"

"Yes, miss."

"Thank you so much."

"Of course."

As I stepped back out into the plaza I realized that my mistake should have been obvious. What business could be conducted at this time of day? The heat was annihilating. Another cab took me back to the hotel.

Back in my room again, empty-handed, I lay on the bed and stared at the ceiling fan for a while. The breeze from the balcony turned the blades. I kept losing the thread of this day. It was hard work avoiding my own doubts. I slept for a few minutes, then woke sweating from a half-dream — the same room I lay in, the same growing heat, but unable to move, as if staked through the chest to the mattress. I saw that what I needed was the pool. I changed into the swimsuit I had packed after so much thought, and went down the stairs again, my sandals loud in the dim, tiled corridor.

There were loungers lined up in ranks around the pool, and I chose one and cranked open the sun umbrella. A few other guests lay here and there, reading paperbacks and newspapers. A child squatted over a busy line of ants that issued from a crack in the concrete pool deck. Spindly date palms reached into a relentless sky. The woman who had come with my breakfast appeared and asked if I would like anything — *un sándwich, un batido, un traguito, un bocadito, un refresco?* Yes, please, a sandwich and a Coke. She brought me a club sandwich with a pile of potato chips whose grease glittered in the sun. I had expected something more Dominican — a *chimi*, maybe. Always the same confusion, an American traveler failing to understand that customs warp and bend around her. I hadn't realized how hungry I was. I ate my lunch in five minutes and settled back in the lounger with the book I had brought: it was *The Prime of Miss Jean Brodie*, which I reread whenever I was at loose ends.

"So sorry," someone said, in mid-Atlantic English.

A man was perched on the next lounger, leaning toward me, his extended fingers a respectful six inches from my arm.

"A light?" he said.

He was young, about my age, in swimming trunks and an open shirt. He was wearing a silver chain. There was a feeling — something like recognition. I took my

184

lighter from my bag, and from some impulse I leaned over into the space between our chairs and lit his cigarette for him. He laughed. "Chivalry isn't dead," he said. That was it — he was queer, I thought. Probably. He settled back into the blue shade under his umbrella, looking pleased with his cigarette, with his own outstretched legs, perhaps with having made my acquaintance. "What brings you to Santo Domingo?" he said.

"You're looking at it," I said.

He smiled, glancing around the pool deck. "It's not bad for the price, is it?"

"I've got no complaints."

"I stayed here once before. The woman who runs it is a sweetheart." He unfolded a *Miami Herald* that had been resting on the table between our chairs, and I returned to my book, obscurely reassured. He seemed like someone I might know at home. Mrs. Spark was saying something devastating about Miss Brodie. Two teenage girls had gotten into the pool, self-conscious in their swimsuits, alternately holding their bodies as if for a photograph and trying to bend and slip sideways to hide them; once they were up to their necks they relaxed and the air filled with their conversation, which was in French. Miss Brodie said, "Give me a

185

girl at an impressionable age, and she is mine for life." I had taken a vacation with my mother to Puerto Rico when I was fourteen and I remembered being this way around the pool, abruptly too tall, not yet in possession of a figure but knowing it was coming, already the recipient of hooded looks and shouted commentary from passing cars back in Chevy Chase. My mother had let me buy a swimsuit from the ladies' department instead of junior miss at Hecht's, which meant that it had a complicated foam-rubber structure inside "for support," and she studiously avoided looking at me whenever I wore it. I had felt like there were spotlights on me on the beach, a feeling that I both hated and loved. My father had been dead two years by then, and my mother and I revolved around each other cautiously. I talked with my best friend, Joanne, about our futures: we would finish school and find an apartment together in the city; she would paint and I would get a job in an office and pay the rent. It was funny now, looking back, this little lesbian fantasy hiding in plain sight. Joanne must have felt some of it too, whatever she said later. The last time I was in Chevy Chase, during that visit to my mother, I ran into a classmate from B-CC at the grocery while I was out buying ground beef, and she told me that Joanne had married a navy man and lived in Annapolis with their two little girls.

CHAPTER 13

I ran into the man again later, in the lobby. He was at a pay phone by the stairs, flustered, reading numbers aloud from a scrap of paper in his hand. I wanted to use the phone myself. I waited in a chair nearby.

"No, routing number," he was saying. "R-o-u-t —" He stopped, searching the ceiling. "Ah, número de — no es el número de la cuenta. Es el número de — de —"

"Ruta," I said, taking mercy on him.

He looked over, frenzied. "What?"

"It's *número de ruta.*"

He repeated that into the phone, apparently with success. He finished his call, looking calmer, and then came over to my chair. "Thanks," he said. "I was spinning in circles."

"Not at all," I said. I didn't want to make my call with other people around — it was an old habit. I thought about coming down to do it later.

"Your Spanish is good," he said.

I laughed. "You've only heard three words."

"But I can tell!" He folded the paper and put it back in his shirt pocket. "I'm a reporter. It's hard enough to get them to pay you when you're in New York. Go in the field and suddenly no one knows how to use Western Union."

"Oh," I said, and then, because it seemed harmless, "I live in New York too."

"Oh, lovely," he said, and leaned over to offer his hand. "I'm Nick."

I took it. "Anne. What are you reporting on?"

"Economic redevelopment."

"Yours?"

He laughed. "The Dominican Republic's."

"Huh. So how's it going?"

"I wish I knew." A woman came into the lobby accompanied by the hotel's overburdened bellhop, who was guiding a luggage rack. We watched him negotiate the foyer, concentrating fiercely, while the wheels of the rack all turned in different directions. "It's just that people don't want to talk to me."

"No?"

"People tend to get in trouble around here for giving their opinions."

"I see."

In the evening, after I had had dinner at a cheap place around the corner and come back to read in my room, there was a knock at the door.

"It's Nick," called a muffled voice. "Sorry to intrude."

I undid the chain and swung open the door. "Oh, hello!"

He was dressed up, and he smelled like sandalwood.

"Well, look at you," I said. "How'd you find my room?"

"I asked downstairs. Is that forward?" he said. "Listen, I'm going out to Club Florida tonight and — well, it's just nicer to have company, isn't it?"

I wondered if he had spotted me the way I had spotted him. Something in his manner did suggest that this was not a date but a performance of a date that could amuse us both. I laughed. "Well sure, that is a little forward."

"Are you busy? Or too tired? I understand. It's only — for single men — at clubs like Florida, it's easier to be in a pair."

"Is that right?"

He shrugged apologetically. I considered it. He looked hopeful and it had been a long time since I'd gone dancing. "Give me a minute to think over my clothes," I said. "I'll meet you downstairs."

"Terrific," he said.

I looked through the things I had brought, which were already crumpled, even though I had gone to the trouble of unpacking them and putting them away in the bureau in the room. I had brought a yellow minidress with some funny beading around the collar, which I had bought in a moment of exuberance the summer before and had been unsure of ever since; it seemed about right for this. In the mirror it strove for an effect that was geometric and minimal, an ancient rune in the form of a dress, and almost made it. My hair was too curly for the dress: it didn't strive for anything in particular, but there we were. I pushed it out of my face with a white headband. Max, I thought, would have had white eyeliner. I could see her in my clothes, clear as day, standing next to me in the hotel room. I could see how she would finish it, pull it off. I could see the shoes she would wear. She always looked like she was in a movie. Where was she tonight? I blotted my lipstick and put on some clacking bracelets. Maybe she wondered where I was right now, and I wanted to have a good answer.

Nick was waiting in the lobby. "Well, hello!" he said, looking over from the conversation he was having with the night girl at the front desk, who was pink from talking to him. "Look at you, a total doll."

"Thank you."

"I thought we could walk. It's only a few blocks. Unless that's — God, how classless. I'll get us a cab —"

"We can walk!"

"Que la pasen bien," said the girl at the desk, her eyes darting back and forth between us.

Club Florida was resplendent on a corner, outlined and buzzing with neon tubes, an ornate facade rising and losing itself in the dark above the colored lights. Velvet ropes stretched down both sidewalks. A policeman in a uniform that bagged at the knees stood in the intersection in front, directing columns of traffic. The cars dawdled in the crossing to scan the hopefuls clinging to each other in front of the club. We joined the line, and I could see why Nick had wanted to bring a woman. Young men on their own were chased to the back of the line by a contemptuous wave from the bouncers; cigarette girls in garters lingered back there, making half-hearted runs at them. "You know your way around this place," I said.

"It's my second trip here since the summer. I'm starting to pick some things up."

"How long did you stay the first time?"

"A month or so."

"And what did you learn?"

He glanced at me. Ahead of us, the doors opened, and a forceful merengue flooded into the street and then was gone again. "What a question," he said. "There's no quick answer to that."

"Well, take your time then."

He laughed. "I'll get there." He looked idly up into the dark. "It's a small island, you know? I didn't realize before I came how a man like Trujillo could be everywhere. And he was everywhere. People kept saying things to me — one man said, 'If you made a joke about Trujillo on the bus, the police would be waiting for you at home.' And now that's all over, but . . ." He shrugged. "But it's not over."

"So it's hard to get interviews?"

"It's hard to know what's happening economically. The reports are all good. The reports are beautiful. But no one really knows. They set up their own rating companies and rate their own bonds. I need to get out into the country and see the cane fields and the coffee and cocoa plantations.

There's a nickel mine I want to see." He fell quiet as if aware again of the line, the giddy partygoers ahead and behind.

"Maybe this isn't the place to talk about it," I said.

"Maybe not. Hard to imagine anyone in this crowd is on the clock, though." The couple in front of us was arguing, the woman's sparkling purse swinging as she declaimed; the couple behind us had fallen into a slow-moving embrace that did not bear inspection.

"Do you go out much in New York?" I said.

He held my look and winked. "Not to this kind of place."

"I see."

"I thought you might."

A final settling in occurred. I stood a little closer to him.

In twenty minutes we were ushered inside, into an atmosphere that was both expansive and stifling. To our left was a bar where uniformed cocktail waitresses alighted and departed, bearing trays. They looked martial and secretarial at once, in short skirts and jackets with epaulets, fabric that glittered darkly in the low light. In front of us stretched a sea of small tables that ended at the shore of an immense and crowded dance floor. We stood still, taking it all in. It had been a theater once, I could see now, one of the old movie palaces from the thirties. I had seen similar ones in New York. The ceiling arched high above us in the dark, painted with geometric shapes that radiated out from the center, art nouveau lozenges becoming Islamic loops and curves. It had faded and there were patches of paint missing, but it was so far away that it could be forgiven, as if the ceiling were subject to distant processes in which human custodians could not be expected to intervene. A band in green tuxedos played on an ample stage at the back of the room, overhung by golden curtains. I watched the dancers. They were good, the place was full of people who knew how to dance, and they had none of the adolescent irony, the protective self-consciousness seen on rock-and-roll dance floors in clubs in New York. Their faces were serious, their hands held high, and they danced navel to navel, breaking apart when the song ended to laugh and applaud. Nick leaned over. "You see how the men keep their shoulders so straight?" he said. "That's because soldiers used to dance merengue with rifles on their backs."

"Is that true?"

"I don't know, but people keep saying it to me."

It seemed hopeless to get a table. Not all of them were occupied by couples, I saw now. There were groups of men at larger ones that ringed the dance floor and lined the bar, their shoulders forward, turning drinks in their hands. They were in uniform. Nick took my hand and towed me around the perimeter of the room, toward a smaller bar not flocked with waitresses, where he ordered us champagne.

"Who are they?" I said, nodding to a table nearby, where three men sat smoking cigars, their hats on, while a cocktail waitress stood just out of range. There were dozens of these men, clustered here and there in the huge ballroom, a few dancing, the flats of their caps visible at a distance, one or two talking to women in the skittish crowds that waited for turns at the edge of the dance floor, but most brooding in the lamplight, smoking, surveying the room.

"How'd they get past those bouncers with so many men?" I said.

Nick executed a flicker of a salute over the rim of his champagne glass. "They're the army," he said. "Some are police. They go where they want."

I felt tension across my rib cage. "They

seem to like this place."

"It's one of their favorites."

I watched him, wondering why he would choose a club like this. The table closest to us were armed: the men leaned heavily on their elbows, and I could see pistols below the hems of their jackets. Their waitress came close to set their drinks on the table, and the tallest of the men put his hand around her thigh as if it were a lamppost. She ignored him.

"Do you dance?" Nick said.

"Not like this crowd."

"Give it a try."

We set our empty glasses on the bar, and he led me to the dance floor. We squared up and I presented my hand. I felt safer here, in the throng of dancers. We were both good at play-acting — of course we were. How many straight dances like this had each of us dodged and weaved through?

"You ever taken a lesson?" he said.

"Just what they made us do in PE." I could remember the time signature, but not the steps, exactly. I watched his feet and tried to mirror them. "Just follow," he said. There was a kind of lightness on the ball of the foot that helped. I wasn't a bad dancer, just ignorant. Nick put his hand low on my hip, directing me, and this was familiar too, the way gay men would sometimes handle women casually, pushing through crowds at the bars without appearing to notice whether they were among friends or strangers.

"There, you're getting it," he said. He lifted and turned my hand, and I did a little spin. We danced until we were hot, and then had more champagne. An older man asked me to dance, nodding at Nick, who nodded back, and we swam out a few paces into the crowd. He was a very good dancer, able to anticipate and compensate for my mistakes. I was a little giddy. We circled the floor twice and then he relinquished me to Nick again with a smile. The band took a break; an old recording crackled out of hidden speakers while they loosened their collars at the edge of the stage. I went to the ladies' room, a shocking shift in color and light, a large gray-tiled room like you might have found in a train station, with an old woman brooding over a basket of hand towels at the far end of the sinks. Women trooped in and out of the stalls, flushed and chattering, rearranging their dresses, patting at their damp faces, leaning in goggle-eyed to the mirrors to reapply their lipstick and mascara. When I came out again, I couldn't find Nick. I was untroubled; I ordered another champagne, enjoying how cheap it was, and accepted an invitation from a young man with a sheen of sweat on his upper lip, who was pained and heated and lacked the grace of my previous partner. As the song ended he pressed his hand against the small of my back and stared into my eyes. My confidence in my performance wavered. I couldn't remember how I used to extricate myself from men like this. I had once been able to do it so quickly and sweetly that hardly anyone got angry with me. I patted his arm and hurried away, but I could feel him staring at my back.

Now I wished in earnest that I knew where Nick was. I was hungry and my feet were starting to throb. I walked the perimeter of the room, where women conferred in the shadows and waitresses stood back to rest. I didn't see him anywhere. I found a chair that was stranded by itself and sat for a while, waving off an invitation or two to dance. It must have been getting close to one o'clock. It had been a long day and I could tell that I was very tired, but I floated above the fatigue, like a balloon.

An inexplicable current of cool air led me finally to a set of double doors on the far side of the dance floor, through which I could see the dark blue of the night outside.

I stepped through into a patio surrounded by a tall fence. Wicker chairs were arranged in clusters, and groups of people stood talking and laughing in the dark. The air smelled like the ocean. I wondered where we were. The sky was open above us. Nick was standing off to the left, talking closely with a man.

I was embarrassed, as if I had already interrupted. I was searching for the handle of the door and thinking of calling a cab when Nick spotted me. "Anne!" he called genially. I turned around and pretended to have just seen him. It was while I was faking this expression that I saw the man was in uniform.

"Annie, this is Captain Arroyo," he said in Spanish, and then both men laughed, as if this formality were a joke in light of their long and intimate friendship. "Marcelo," said the captain, kissing my cheek. He smelled like rum. Nick was weaving happily on his feet. I wondered if he was nervy enough to be trying to pick up this soldier. There were some who were. The man had a soft Rudolph Valentino face. He had removed his hat and his damp hair was standing up, as if he had been running his hands through it. For a fraction of a second after the greeting kiss he lingered near my face, suspended in the dark.

"Marcelo knows a quieter place," Nick said.

CHAPTER 14

The quieter place had no neon lights and no marquee over the sidewalk. We stepped out of a cab in front and I tried to memorize the street, to make out the signs at the corners, the storefronts (shutters down, unlit) across the way, but there was nothing to catch on to. In the cab I had tried to mark each turn we had taken but had lost track; the streets were narrow in this part of town and we had stopped and reversed twice when blocked by the tedious inching of a night bus. I felt sober because I was nervous, but I could tell that I wasn't thinking all that fast, and the champagne and the long hours were weighing on me. Marcelo had assumed the role of my chaperone, and helped me onto the sidewalk. It was all campy, his intercession between me and every door we had encountered since leaving Club Florida, but I doubted that he found it so himself. Nick was perpetually

202

half a step away from him on the other side, cheerful, apparently inexhaustible, his collar undone.

Marcelo went ahead of us to talk to the doorman, who stood under a light at the side of the unmarked door. Nick lit a cigarette.

"You're in love?" I said.

He smiled.

"This isn't New York," I said. "He's not some kid on a weekend pass."

"He seems interested in you," Nick said.

"He's not very perceptive."

"He's nice though, isn't he?"

But Marcelo was coming back, grinning, clasping his hands, and we both stopped talking. "You're my guests," he said. "It's all understood."

Irritated, I followed them inside. It was a long, low room, a wash of black interrupted only by well-shaded lamps in leather banquettes. At the far end, a girl with honey-brown hair stood illuminated like the Virgin behind a shining bar. She was holding a shaker with both hands, her nails were painted and she wore a lot of bracelets, and for an instant she was Max; then she turned to pour the drink and I saw that her hair was a wig, and she was a stranger again. There were no other women in the place.

I shouldn't have come. I was either an unwilling trois in this ménage or Nick had dangerously misunderstood Marcelo, and in both cases, I would have been better off back at the hotel hours ago. It was just that Nick felt like an ally and I was alone on this island with half a plan. We chose a banquette, Marcelo crowded in beside me and Nick sat across from us, and a waiter came to take our order. Marcelo asked for a round of something for the table, a name I didn't recognize, and the waiter returned with three glasses of something dark. Nick launched into a raucous, serviceable Spanish. He wanted to know where Marcelo had grown up and what position he had played on his district-champion baseball team and what had happened to the high school *novia* he had almost married and where his dear old parents were living now. Marcelo answered all questions, elaborated, became wistful. Another round of drinks came. Marcelo's military posture was buckling, his elbows were on the table, ash from his waving cigarette landed on the silky surface of his drink. I had stopped drinking mine. I longed for a plate of chicken and mashed potatoes.

"Three generations," Marcelo said. "We're all army men."

"No such pressure for me," Nick said, winking. "My father's an accountant."

Marcelo's thigh was pressed against mine under the table, but it was hard to say if it was on purpose. I could feel his weight. I withdrew into the corner of the booth, and he corrected for the lack of support, tipping the other way, and then looked at me over the horizon of his own shoulder as if he had just caught me doing something flirtatious.

"My father was a magazine editor," I said, for no particular reason.

"A scurrilous profession," Nick said in English.

"My father was a colonel," Marcelo said. "I serve in his old command. But he's retired now. Sits and looks at the water all day."

"What command is that, Captain?" said Nick.

"Intelligence."

For me there was a shift, as if the film in the projector had just skipped off the reel. Then it caught and held again, and I pretended to yawn. My body had gone rigid. I took a deep breath disguised by a sip of the drink and willed my arms and legs to relax again. I felt a righteous fury at Nick that would have to wait awhile before it could do anything much.

"Intelligence!" Nick said. "That's the hardest to get into. I had a friend who did it. A guy from around here. He spent years training."

Marcelo nodded modestly. He was trying to light another cigarette, but his depth perception was gone. Nick took the lighter from him. He wouldn't look at me.

"My father practically ran the CEFA," Marcelo said, leaning back now, his cigarette lit. "He had lunch every month with Trujillo. General Wessin would visit our house at the beach when he went on vacation." Sadness or anger came over him. He sat up straight. "The Americans betrayed him. He did everything for them when the marines came, and they threw him away like trash."

"What did they do to him?" Nick said.

"They exiled him. They came with guns and took him to the airport and put him on a plane to Miami. He had to leave everything behind; his house, his dogs." He leaned back, looking up into the low plaster ceiling. "He's a good man. He'll be back."

"You're in the CEFA, then?" Nick said.

"No, no. They took it apart after he left." He blinked, very slowly. I thought he might not open his eyes again, but he did. "They took it apart. But we remember. All of us who trained there."

"You remember?"

His gaze traveled down in no great hurry from the ceiling and alighted on Nick's face. He smiled. "We remember all the old tricks," he said.

So much of the work is in trying to get close. But what I had taken a long time to learn, and would not now forget, was how dangerous it was to get closer than you meant to. I stared at Nick until he looked at me, and then I fell sleepily against the padded back of the booth. "I'm too tired," I said. "And I'm hungry. I've got to go home."

"Ah," Nick said, touching his hair. "Well —"

"Sweetheart, don't go," Marcelo said, drifting my way again, blocking the light. "It's early."

"But it's *late,*" I said, smiling.

He put his arm around me. It was heavy and his shirtsleeve was damp. "Some man is missing you?"

"Let me out," I said. "I've had too much to drink." I put a hand over my mouth and hunched my shoulders. Marcelo slid rapidly out of my way and I was free, dragging my pocketbook after me.

"I'd better take the lady home," Nick was saying.

I made it to the bar in a few long steps.

"Sweetheart," I said to the girl in the wig, and she turned as if revolving on a stand, like a ballerina in a music box. "You have the number of a cab?"

Nick caught up with me while I was waiting outside.

"Look," he said.

"I don't need any explanations," I said. "I'm just leaving."

"It's a little bit complicated," he said.

"It's none of my business."

Nick glanced back toward the door of the club.

"What, is he coming?" I said.

"No, he found a friend in there."

"A second friend, you mean."

He turned back, listing under the weight of an apologetic smile. "I can't imagine what you're thinking."

"I'm thinking they killed a lot of people, Nick, and are probably still killing a lot of people, and I have no idea what you think two queers from New York are going to get out of hanging around with one of them."

A cab rounded the corner and, to my huge relief, nosed up to the curb in front of us. Nick darted out and opened the door for me.

"After you," he said.

"Oh, are you getting in this cab too?" But

I didn't stop him. He went around to the other side and climbed in. I gave the address of the hotel. He waited a few minutes, until the car was humming along a stretch of highway that fronted the beach, the perfect blackness of the ocean filling the windows on the right side, and then spoke quietly in English.

"I'm here for the reason I said," he said. "I'm a reporter. But I'm not looking for a story on the economy."

Nick's room was two floors below mine, facing the same way, the balcony putting him even with a sign on the discount department store across the way, so that DAMAS — CABALLEROS — NIÑOS glared hopefully in four-foot letters through his French doors. I had agreed to come only because he said he had a leftover sandwich there that I could have. I collapsed in a chair and he handed it to me, wrapped in foil.

"So what is it, then?" I said. "What's the story you're after?"

"I want to find out what happened to Trujillo's machine after Trujillo died."

"Isn't it everywhere you look?"

"I mean, Balaguer is part of it himself. But he claims he took apart the police state and I don't think he did. I think the secret police are still very active."

I was still angry, although I was pleased with the sandwich: layers of pork, with pickles. "Doesn't everybody know that already?" I said.

"Dominicans know that. I don't think Americans do."

Why did that make me so sad? I looked at the LL in CABALLEROS. I had been awake in the night for so long and it would still be hours before the sun came up. I tried to recall what I had understood about politics when I was twenty years old, twenty-two, before all this. I could hardly remember. Some vague symbolic nonsense, a schematic of the world that now looked like the backdrop of a child's play.

"So that's why you chose that place," I said.

He had lit another cigarette and was searching in a drawer. I thought I saw embarrassment; he could have looked at me, but didn't. "Yes."

"I thought you wanted to pick up soldiers," I said.

"Well, I would have settled for that."

I snorted. Nick gave up on the drawer and went out to the balcony, returning with an ashtray.

"You could get into trouble," I observed.

He sat in the other chair, next to a floor lamp with a parrot painted on the shade. He rested one ankle on his knee and looked down at his dress sock for a long time.

"It gets to be a habit," he said finally.

"Oh? You've done this kind of thing before?"

"I spent a little time in Guatemala after the coup in '63."

I waited for him to go on, but that was all he said. I thought of Argentina, the crowd of people at the ferry terminal the day the tanks rolled into Buenos Aires. The far-reaching and heavy and vibrating lack of surprise. A few soldiers I had seen that evening, drinking toasts to each other in a bar on Carlos Calvo, as if a pitched battle had just been won or a wedding celebrated. The president had been an old man with gentle manners, and they had merely sent him away in a car with a couple of guards. It was the ease of it that had shocked me in the end, the way a veil of procedure had just fallen away. The new president put on all his medals, held a press conference, and then threw himself a parade.

"I know a man who was in the Sierra Maestra with Castro," Nick said. "A correspondent for the *Washington Post.*" There was a sheen of jealousy over it. He actually put his chin on his fist, looking out toward the French doors.

"Real action for once," I said, unkindly.

He glanced at me. "I guess this all looks a little perverse to most people. Chasing this kind of thing around."

"It's a living." Unexpectedly, I felt a brief desire to tell him the truth about my life, or at least I imagined what it might be like if I did. But it passed. I ate the last bits of the sandwich and crumpled the foil.

"I really apologize," he said. "To tell you the truth, even though I went out hoping I would meet somebody useful, I didn't expect it to work out — well, quite as well as it did. I didn't think I would involve you in anything. A total stranger! It was stupid."

He looked sincere, even upset. "Well," I said. I put the ball of foil on the end table and stood up to go. "No harm done."

In the morning I was ready and waiting outside the Palacio Municipal when the massive doors creaked open at a quarter to nine. The square was quiet at that time, the palacio casting a long shadow across it, the leaves of jacaranda picked out in the rich light. There was a flutter of secretaries rising from the benches when the bolts were shot, and I watched them stream past me

212

into the dark of the building.

I chose the same window and the same clerk as the day before. He left an office boy to steward his chair and led me up a flight of unlit stairs into a large, high-ceilinged room, guarded by a woman at a green desk. She was backed by battalions of filing cabinets that stretched to distant windows. It reminded me of an obscure wing of a research library uptown where I had met Jane once to take her out to lunch. The same helpless sense of history at our heels, of there being too many things in the world that were irreplaceable but not in use, of time doggedly gaining on us. She had wanted a first edition of something. A book of poems. She was bright-eyed when I came to get her because she had found it and there had been an inscription on the title page: *To my sweetheart, Christmas 1837.* I remembered the white gloves they made her wear, flitting in the bad light.

"She's looking for a license," the clerk said to the woman at the desk, who looked startled, as if this were a day she had prepared for but had hoped would never come. She cleared a newspaper and a piece of lacework off the table and put on her glasses.

"The name is Ibarra," I said. "They were

married fifteen or twenty years ago." A guess.

"Fifteen or twenty?"

"I'm not sure."

She looked at the clerk who had brought me. He shrugged. "What is your purpose?" she said.

"They're family," I said.

"Hmm," she said. "It would be better to be certain of the year."

"It would be," I said amiably.

The clerk was already thudding down the stairs behind me. The woman stood and entered the ranks of filing cabinets, and I waited at her desk. There were no visitors' chairs. I could hear drawers opening and closing in the far reaches of the room. Ten minutes passed, fifteen. My feet were beginning to ache, and it was hot. A fan rotated on a stand nearby, making a lot of noise and moving the air only a little. I thought about sitting in the woman's chair, but guessed that it would be an affront. I paced. A cat I hadn't noticed stood up on a windowsill, stretched, and dropped down to the floor, and I spent some time chatting with it and petting it. The sound of drawers on rusted slides moved closer, then retreated again. Thirty minutes had passed when the woman returned, holding a manila folder, smiling.

It was them: Dionisio Domínguez y Ibarra wed Altagracia Lopez y Centurion in the cathedral of Santa María la Menor on January 28, 1950. The date caught me. "Their anniversary just passed," I said. My eyes stung. I glanced up at the woman, embarrassed, and saw that she was searching my face. "My aunt and uncle," I said.

"Are they living?" she said softly.

There it was, the newlyweds' address, as I had hoped: Hacienda la Romana, Avenida de las Caobas, Prov. de San Cristóbal.

"Yes," I said. "Still living."

CHAPTER 15

I needed a driver. I went back to my room at the hotel and changed into an outfit that looked Californian to me, a dress with a complicated print and sandals. I put most of the cash I had left in the safe. I went out to the balcony and smoked a cigarette and had another stare down with the casino girl on the billboard.

I worried that there would be no one there. I hoped for servants who could tell me something — anything — about where the Ibarras had gone. I felt hot. I had heard that a lot of the old families kept a place in the capital but really lived out there, on haciendas. Maybe this was the home the boy thought of, more than wherever they had lived in Santo Domingo when the war started. There was a buzz in the air like static, which I recognized from old times: it was fear, the trace that fear left when you pushed it out of your mind. I took the camera case out of my suitcase and loaded the gun inside with the bullets I had brought in an empty cold cream jar. I disliked guns but would have liked the idea of this trip into the country even less without it. I had packed it to give me courage. A gun rearranged things around itself.

I stood over the pad of hotel stationery on the side table for a few minutes, thinking, and then picked up my purse and went to the door. I stopped there and closed my eyes and tried to think. There was a lightness I distrusted in my arms and shoulders, in my hands wrapped around my bag. I went back to the table and wrote a few lines on the pad, folded the note, and sealed it in a cream-colored envelope. On the outside I wrote *Nick*.

In the lobby I asked the girl at the desk for a driver for the day and waited in a low vinyl chair while she called someone whom I understood to be, from her muttered phone conversation, a cousin of hers.

"Miguel will be here in thirty minutes," she said to me after she hung up.

An hour passed. I read most of the paper while I waited. Strikes, robberies, murders. An editorial about the sanctity of Dominican motherhood. Miguel appeared at one o'clock, a pockmarked young man in jeans, and greeted his cousin with a kiss on the cheek. I hoisted myself out of the chair and came to the desk.

"I'm Anne," I said.

He nodded but hardly looked at me. Up close he had a petrochemical smell, like he had been interrupted while under a car, and seemed shy. I checked my bag again to be sure I had everything I needed and then slid the envelope to the girl.

"Please give this to the gentleman in room 302," I said.

The sea glittered as we drove out of Santo Domingo. It was the dry season, someone had told me. The car was an old Ford, and Miguel drove it carefully but fast, doing more with the clutch than was really necessary, patting the dash when the engine complained. We passed a monument of some kind in a plaza, a peristyle with smooth white columns and a series of flags; it was gone before I could get a good look at it. This was such an old city, but the parts that I had seen were so new, a profusion of whitened concrete, brightly printed advertisements, fresh asphalt. The salt wind kept the trees from growing high near the beach, and that made them seem new as well. The beach spread away to our left, strewn with sunbathers and umbrellas. Shaved-ice carts wobbled across the sand. On the right we passed low warehouses, the lots filled with row upon row of battered trucks, and then a collection of shops in primary colors with their names painted in white on the walls — ROPA, ZAPATOS, BIENES PARA LA CASA, FERRETERÍA, GOMERÍA, CARNECERÍA, PANADERÍA. At intervals, immense hotels interrupted all this ordinary human activity.

"Have you always lived in Santo Domingo?" I said to Miguel in Spanish.

He glanced at me in the rearview mirror and then looked away, as if he had just confirmed that I was talking to someone else.

"In Santo Domingo?" I tried again. "Have you always lived here?"

"Oh," he said. "Yes."

"It's beautiful," I said. We were separated from the beach at that moment by a line of palms, and through their trunks the water was electric blue, with a gentle surf breaking like a crust of sugar against the beach. A woman was selling plastic flowers from a cart on the median of the highway and the sunlight made them gorgeous, poignant: bundles of fake lilies and roses in yellow and pink, wrapped in green cellophane.

219

"It reminds me a little of Los Angeles," I said.

In the mirror I could see him frowning at the road. On an impulse I said, "I wish my husband could have come with me on this trip, but his mother is sick. We usually travel together."

An expression passed over his face that I could only describe as relief. It seemed obvious then, his shy silence since the hotel. My solitude was too much. It was indecent. I should have worn a ring.

"You've been here before?" he said, relaxing into his seat.

"No, never," I said.

Congestion at a traffic circle, and then a shift, the city thinning. The hotels stopped appearing. The shops remained, and houses filled in the gaps, crowded together to make corrugated rooflines that bent and met at angles. As these houses grew smaller and then farther apart, the flora of the island began to overwhelm them. Piles of vines spilled over walls, trailing orange flowers. Chickens scratched warily on the shoulder of the highway. The land was flat here, the horizon close; whatever was close to the highway obscured everything behind.

It was two o'clock by my watch. Miguel turned the radio dial until he found a baseball game and settled in. He looked at me once more in the mirror. "Los Angeles, yes?" he said.

"Yes, but I'm from New York before that."

"Oh, New York! I have cousins there. Yankees fan?"

"Mets!"

He clucked disapprovingly and laughed. My father had been an Orioles fan. I remembered him on spring Saturdays, out in the yard with a pair of clippers, pruning the delicate Japanese maples he had planted in islands of soft mulch, listening to the Orioles game on a portable radio propped up in the grass. Or working on the car in the drive, wearing his single pair of blue jeans, which he owned for those occasions, with the car radio tuned to the WQBR broadcast. He was a genteel kind of person, unsure with other men, slow to join in jokes, but he had liked baseball. By the time I was old enough to understand where he had actually come from, the frontier where he had grown up, and wonder about the discrepancy between that place and this bespectacled editor with his complete set of Tolstoy and his ironed neckties, he was already gone. From his brother I heard a childhood story about him killing a rattlesnake with a chisel when it surprised them in the barn one day. "That was all he had in his hand," my uncle said. Little things — the hysterical murmur of the color commentary on the radio — brought him back so clearly that he could have been sitting beside me in the car, and yet he answered no questions, offered no explanations. The dead linger, they stay with us, but they don't speak, and anyone who says different is selling something.

Félix had brought the cat home, which made it his. Or really, the cat had followed him home from the restaurant on a Friday night, and he had let it come into the big cold kitchen of the house on the hill and given it a meatball that he had mashed flat with a fork. It was a black cat with yellow eyes. You could feel its backbone when you petted it, but it didn't seem sick, or weak, or even all that worried about anything. Dean, who slept in the living room, said that it was a tom and it would piss everywhere. Félix said it wouldn't. Later he had seen Dean sitting and petting the cat so he must not have been too annoyed about it.

"What's his name?" Charlie had said. He was one of the older boys who slept in the warmer bedroom. Félix mostly stayed out of his way.

222

"I don't know," Félix said.

"What do you mean, you don't know? So you give him one."

But Félix couldn't think of anything that didn't seem too childish. Naming a cat felt like playing pretend. He wished the cat had come with a name, somehow. He sat with him in the cold front bedroom and the cat nudged and nosed him and climbed into his lap, and turned around twice before lying down, settling over his crossed ankles and his sneakers, which were already starting to fall apart.

Rubén, Félix thought. The name of an old yellow dog he had known once on the island. The groundskeeper's dog, who walked around with a stick in his mouth all the time.

In the morning Félix gave Rubén another meatball, and when he left for work the cat was asleep on a chair in the living room. When he returned that night, he searched the house and found the cat in a closet that had been left open, on a forgotten coat with the lining torn out. A week went by like that, then another week. Félix started going to the five and dime at the bottom of the hill and buying cans of cat food. He kept them in the pantry, which was otherwise empty of anything but flyspecks and old mousetraps.

The house was dirty and bare, except for the mattresses upstairs and a few chairs salvaged from the street, but it felt more comfortable with the cat around. The cat often stood by the door and looked up at Félix, serene but insistent; it amazed Félix that the cat was so sure he could make himself understood. If he opened the door, Rubén would slip out into the dark yard. Félix sometimes fell asleep in the armchair in the front room, waiting to hear him come back. If he went up to bed instead, he often found the cat in his room in the morning, let in by one or another of the boys who had come in late.

What Félix really wanted was to keep Rubén inside and close by all the time, so it was hard to let him out. One day, a day off, he refused to do it. Rubén paced and complained. Félix told him to hush. He walked away, hoping Rubén would follow him like he usually did, but Rubén crouched on the rubber mat at the door and wouldn't move. Félix hauled him away and shut him in the hall closet. He sat in the chair by the window and listened to Rubén calling in the dark. There was something vibrating in Félix's chest; his eyes skipped around when he tried to read. He was alone in the living room.

"Hush," he said. "Don't I feed you?"

But he was crying. There was no one to see. Rubén only got louder. Félix dropped the book and opened the hall closet, his face wet and red, and the cat spilled out, looking up steadily at him with his yellow eyes. He bumped his head against Félix's shin and did a figure eight between his feet.

Just a few days after that, Félix didn't see Rubén in the morning before he left for work. He tried not to think about it all day while he carried bins of dishes back and forth and unloaded the scalding Hobart. But Rubén still wasn't there when he got home, and he didn't come the next morning either, or that night or the day after that. Félix could see now that the forgiveness he had felt when he freed the cat from the hall closet had been provisional and that he had failed to show that he deserved it. He crumpled when he thought of it, so he had to stop thinking of it. He cried only on his walk home, safely alone in the dark, before the scarce lights of the big house came into view.

"San Cristóbal," Miguel said, pointing out the window at an exit sign. In the distance, a low range of mountains rose up, dense with green-gray forest. "It's the capital of the province." The gas stations and shops had thickened again along the sides of the road, but the city of San Cristóbal itself was not visible as we passed. The landscape here had more turns and folds, and things were hidden. "Trujillo was born here," he said.

"Ah," I said. It seemed safer not to comment further. "So we're close?" I said instead.

"Yes. They're family, these people you're going to see?"

"No, this is for business."

"Business?" His eyebrows went up. I glanced at the gold-washed case in my bag with the business cards in it.

"Did you see *Zombie Woman*?" I hazarded.

"Yes, of course!" He lit up. "They made it here! That was a great movie."

I had seen the placards for the movie still up near the hotel, and someone had proudly told me this already, that it was filmed in a beach town an hour or two east of the capital.

"Yes, I work for the studio that made that movie," I said. "When they need a place to make a movie, they send me out to find one. We need a mansion. And they like to work here on the island."

"What about your husband?"

"He works for the studio too. That's how we met. I was his assistant."

He nodded, satisfied. He stopped for gas and I watched him conferring over the road map with the man in the shop. A few miles later, we took an exit by a fruit stand selling guavas and descended on a narrow road. After the speed and the open sky of the highway, this was an abrupt change, the road spotted with potholes that had been filled with gravel, the forest encroaching on small houses and pens of animals on either side. Three dogs loped alongside the car, barking, darting forward when we slowed to inch across a stretch where the asphalt was in pieces, and then falling back again as the road grew smoother and began to curve upward. I kept swallowing and touching the sunglasses on my head. The camera case was heavy on my leg and I kept one hand on it. Nothing like going into the woods alone.

"Another ten, twenty minutes," Miguel said, driving now with the road map unfolded on his knee.

The forest was cleared here, and farms appeared on the slopes, small houses among thick rows of coffee bushes and stands of banana trees. A group of children walking along the road broke into a run as the car passed, shrieking and laughing and throwing things after us. Then Miguel turned off to the right and beneath the wheels the pavement went smooth as silk.

"Money," Miguel said, with a little sigh.

"Is this it?" I sat up, peering out the window. Nothing but rows of coffee bushes on either side.

"Yes, Avenida de las Caobas. Must be a private road."

The sky was overcast here in the mountains. I hadn't noticed the change until now. The air was still, the leaves were still; over the fields, birds circled and dove. There was a man out there pointing a rifle at the sky.

The caobas came into view — mahogany trees. We entered an avenue of them, like the live oaks that line the roads to plantations. The roots stood up from the ground, and the trunks were straight and broad, lost in the space above the car. I leaned out the window, looking up into the crowns against the white of the sky. I imagined Altagracia as a young bride, being driven down this avenue on her wedding day. A yellow stucco guardhouse appeared beside an open gate.

Miguel slowed to a stop. I leaned forward in the back seat. He put the car in neutral and set the brake, and I watched him get out and approach the smoked-glass window.

The quiet of the mountain pressed in, even over the idling engine. A breeze moved through the caoba leaves, a faintly oceanic sound. Maybe a warning of rain. Miguel had cupped his hands around his eyes and was trying to see into the guardhouse. He stepped to one side and knocked on a door. I watched it fall open under his hand.

"Señora?" he called back to me, helplessly.

"Let's go on," I said. "Since the gate is open."

We drove through, past a turnoff for a dirt road that led away across a field. I thought of the man with the rifle. The place wasn't empty. But we saw no one now. Lawns opened up on either side of the avenue — lawns that had not been cut in some time. A red clay tennis court, surrounded by low topiary, with the net fallen in. At a turn, a horse stood across the road. It shied back when we stopped, and ambled away through bushes dotted with fruit.

"You're sure there are people here?" Miguel said.

"I don't really know," I said. "I just heard it was a nice estate. Maybe I'm too late."

"People leave, sometimes — they leave suddenly."

The car emerged from the avenue of trees into a circular drive, and the house rose up before us. Miguel and I both sat back involuntarily in our seats. The car coasted to a stop, as if too shy to approach any closer. The yellow stucco of the guardhouse was repeated here, but on a grand scale, fringed with palms, circled by a double row of verandas. Two staircases rose from the ground to meet at the broad front door. Tall casement windows looked down on us; their gaze was chaotic, and I realized while I looked at them that it was because some of the curtains were drawn and some were open or half open, and some were covered with shutters, with no particular pattern. At the far end, one of these shutters hung crookedly from a hinge. A few large and anonymous objects — furniture? — were sheltered in the first-floor veranda, covered with canvas. Concrete urns ran along the front of the house, some empty, some filled with a flowering bush I didn't recognize, some broken, one hosting a ravaged stick netted with spiderwebs.

"Grand people," Miguel said. He turned off the engine, and the ticking as it cooled filled the silence. "But where are they?"

"No way to find out but knock, is there?" I said. I gathered my things together and got out of the car. The heat reasserted itself under the low roof of clouds. I lifted the hair off the back of my neck. The lawn was terraced, the way the English do it, and on the nearest terrace a flock of chickens was scratching in grass that looked incongruous in this riot of nature — the island in general being a place where the earth either burst forth with serrated leaves and vines and flowers or was kept laboriously bare, showing the red dirt. The chickens and their skinny rooster huddled away from me at the sound of the car door closing, making cooing noises of alarm. Off to the left of the circular drive, a goat wearing a bell grazed at the foot of a gazebo that could have housed a modest orchestra.

I climbed the left staircase in front. Water pooled on the steps. The veranda, I saw when I reached the top, was silted in with dead leaves from the tree in front. It had not been swept in a long time. But on a round patio table near the door, an empty bottle of rum, some jam jars, and a mango skin attracted a fresh cloud of flies. I lifted the iron knocker and let it fall twice. There was no answer. I tried again. Over my shoulder, I could see Miguel in the car, leaning on the wheel, looking left and right.

It was at that moment that the man with the rifle walked up the driveway behind the car.

CHAPTER 16

A small woman, her hair cut fashionably short to her jaw-line, wearing a wool coat a few seasons out of date, had been waiting all morning in the hallway outside the coroner's office in the city building on Chambers Street in Manhattan. The building was strange, a labyrinth of veined brown marble, underlit and loud with echoes. Civil servants came and went through a vast atrium, sorting themselves into a warren of cramped, carpeted offices.

She smoked while she waited. There was a machine that gave out numbers, and she held her number on its fragile pink paper in one gloved hand as if she had forgotten it was there. The hallway was cold and she didn't remove her coat or hat.

"You'll have to give us more information," they said at last when her number was called. "This will take a long time, if that's all you have."

"That's all I have," she said. "I'll wait." An accent, a still face.

The man with the rifle walked in no great hurry along the gravel drive and passed the car with a glance at Miguel, who stayed where he was. He came to a stop at the foot of the stairs and looked up at me, tipping the brim of a sun hat out of his eyes to do so.

"You're lost, miss?" he said.

My mouth had gone dry. "No, not lost," I said. I was above him but wished our positions were reversed. There was no obvious way off the porch except down the stairs. "I'm looking for the owners."

"There's no one here to talk to you," he said.

I decided to come down. I did it smiling, watching my feet. "I just want to talk to them about this beautiful place," I said. "I work for a movie studio." I stepped onto the grass, got the cards out of my bag, offered him one. He was standing just too far away to take it, holding the rifle loosely at his side. He was about fifty, weather-beaten, the same height as I was. "They send me out to find places where they can film. My boss is taking meetings back in Santo Domingo but he said he would come out if I found something good. He pays big money to use a place like this." I waved at the facade of the house. "Okay, it needs a little work, but the gardens, the mountain — it's perfect."

He hadn't moved, so I crossed the few feet between us and pressed the card into his hand, beaming. He scratched his forehead. Behind him, I saw Miguel in the car, tense, staring. I watched the man think.

"Well, come in," he said finally.

"Oh, thank you!" I adjusted the strap of the camera case on my shoulder. "I would love to see the inside."

He looked carefully at my face. "You must be thirsty," he said. "If you drove all the way from Santo Domingo."

I concentrated on keeping my face bright, open. "I am, to tell you the truth."

He led me back up the stairs and through the front door, which was decorated with hammered-iron hinges. It creaked open into a tiled two-story foyer. Overcast daylight fell through a transom window and, high above us, a hatch in the roof.

"Oh, lovely," I said.

"This way," he said. Away from the open spaces and windows, the place was dark. There were no lights on. We walked a long hallway, passing a parlor full of old furniture. A cot was unmade in the middle of the grand rug; a pile of water-stained *Vogue* magazines spilled from a chaise longue. The next room was a study with a dark polished desk, on which someone had left a propane bottle and a pair of work gloves.

"Here's the kitchen," he said. It was bright after the hallway, and I squinted. A barefoot woman was standing over a pot at the stove, and she turned and started when I came in, then smoothed her hair back. It was a huge room, with two stoves and deep wooden counters, many windows set open to catch the breeze coming down the mountain, a thick steam in the air from whatever was in the pot, and a collection of damp brassieres and girdles hanging over the high backs of the chairs that lined the worktable.

"Irma," the man said, "the lady comes from a movie studio. She says they'll pay to make a movie here."

"A few scenes of a movie," I said, smiling. "If I can just talk to the owners? The Ibarras, yes?"

"But they're not here," Irma said, dismayed. She looked back and forth between the man and me.

"Not here?" I said.

"Irma, the lady needs a lemonade, she's come a long way," the man said.

235

"Do you know how I could get in touch with them?" I said.

Irma searched in the refrigerator. So the electricity was still on.

"How much money?" the man said abruptly.

"Well, that's for the contract," I said. "But I've seen four hundred a day."

"Four hundred dollars?"

"Sure. And usually a bit extra for expenses. A cleaning crew, a little landscaping." When I was in the midst of a riff, it felt like turning a cartwheel: the same blank concentration. The same tension and smoothness. I was too aware of the heavy camera case on my hip and I deliberately didn't touch it again, didn't glance down at it. Irma had found a bottle of lemonade and was opening it with a church key from a hook on the wall. From outside there was a hiss: through the windows I saw a curtain of soft rain move down the mountain and across the yard, reaching the house with a spattering of drops and a low movement of air. Irma looked up and began to close the window, thought better of it, left it open.

"The señores have gone to New York," she said, turning back to the room again.

"New York?" I tried to take that in. I had come all this way, and they had gone to

New York. Outside the window, the horse we had seen earlier in the road trotted across the lawn, spooked by the change in the weather. A tree full of birds close by chittered and complained. I reached for the right thing to say. "When will they be back?"

She shrugged. The man set the rifle down on the worktable and leaned against the counter, facing me, his arms crossed.

"Did they leave a forwarding address?" I said. Because I was tense and wanted to stand, I pulled out a chair noisily instead and sat in it, leaning on an elbow planted near the rifle, as if I had already forgotten it, as if all I was thinking about was how inconvenient this was.

"We handle the business while they're away," the man said.

"Oh yes?"

"Yes. We handle the money."

"Oh," I said. "I see. But we would need a contract. Without the owners, there's no liability insurance. Think what they could say when they get back!"

Irma said, "They might not get back for a long time."

"They could sue us into the ground," I said, taking a regretful sip of the lemonade. "The studio would never sign off on it."

"We can get you whatever papers you

want," the man said.

I shook my head, pretending not to understand what he meant. "We would have to talk to them. It would all have to be signed, with witnesses. We could send someone to New York, that's not a problem. You just have to —"

"You don't know how things are here," the man said. "We don't know who you are."

"Of course, of course," I said. "I'm only making an offer."

"No, you don't understand." He uncrossed his arms. "We handle the business. If there's money, it goes through us."

"We don't know you," Irma seconded in a soft voice.

"It's not safe dealing with strangers here," the man said. "Maybe you don't know."

"It's the same the world over," I said, and then got up, because I didn't think he was going to give. Maybe knowing that they were in New York was enough. The house was enclosed by rain.

"Irma, show her the upstairs," the man said suddenly.

"The upstairs?" she said.

"You'll see," he said. "It's a beautiful house."

"I can see it is," I said. I had been hot all along, but now I was beginning to feel

238

queasy. I didn't want to go up another set of stairs with this man, or with Irma. "I'm more interested in the grounds. The mountain is what we need."

He hesitated, then nodded. "Irma, show her the grounds."

Irma wiped her hands on a dishcloth and turned down the flame under the pot on the stove. "All right, for a few minutes."

"Don't worry about the pot," the man said. "Salvador will watch it. Where is he, anyway?"

"God knows."

"I'll find him," the man said. "Miss." He nodded at me and went out.

In the quiet after his footsteps faded, Irma and I took a good look at each other. She was middle-aged, her hair black, her arms strong, wearing a housedress.

"It's raining," she said.

"I don't mind," I said. "It's important to see everything."

"But your shoes," she said, distressed, pointing at my sandals, which were flimsy and white.

"It doesn't matter."

"I'll find an umbrella," she said.

We left the kitchen and walked toward the back of the house, down an even dimmer hall. Here there were more signs of life, the elegant rooms that had been kept for entertaining clearly occupied with the work of living. In anticipation of the rain, someone had strung up a rope of laundry down a back stairway. Passing a solarium, we surprised a woman nursing a baby, her feet propped up on a gardener's cart. I wondered how many people were living here. Irma searched in a boot closet and produced an umbrella and a man's rain jacket, which she insisted I put on.

The heat had not broken with the rain and I was stifled in the jacket. We walked out into the lawn. To the left, a set of white steps flanked by urns led down to an empty white pool. What I took at first for an accumulation of dead leaves at the bottom turned out to be half a dozen chickens huddled in the rain. Beyond the pool, the ground sloped upward, and where it could no longer be called a lawn, rows of banana trees were planted, their broad leaves waving softly in the new current of air. At a steeper elevation, the forest began. The mountain breathed over us, whitened by vapor, bare pale branches showing here and there in the dense canopy of leaves. To the right a little two-story cottage sat dark-windowed in its shadow, a lawn jockey by the gravel walk in front. It was out of step with the big house:

white stucco, flat-roofed, without flourishes, like the houses in Santo Domingo. A child's bicycle was overturned under an open shed at the side, among garden equipment stowed out of the weather. "That's where the housekeeper stayed," said Irma.

"How long have the Ibarras been gone?" I said.

She looked at me again, reading me. "A few months now."

So — not long after Mrs. Villanueva died. "And everyone else stayed?"

She shifted away. I shouldn't have said that. "An empty house attracts thieves," she said.

"Right, of course. They must be glad you're here."

She turned toward the back of the big house again. She seemed uneasy and I wanted to get away. I was jumping ahead, thinking how long it would take to nudge this tour back around to the front of the house, back to the car. A bird was calling in the woods, something with a strident voice like a macaw.

"I can't tell you where they are because I don't know," she said abruptly. "But I can tell you who their man was."

"Their man?"

She was shifting from one foot to the

other, clasping her hands. She turned her anxious gaze on me again like a searchlight. "Octavio is stubborn, he doesn't want to say anything. He has a hard head."

"Sure, sure." Now I was looking back too, at the upper windows behind us.

"They know a man in New York. He's the one Dominicans talk to when they need something. People call him El Jabalí."

"What's his real name?"

She shrugged, agitated. "I don't know. But everyone knows him. Every Dominican knows him. He's the one who can get papers."

"The Ibarras didn't have papers?"

"No, their papers were taken after the war. They couldn't travel. Señor Ibarra was a popular man. People talked about him running for president. Balaguer kept them stuck out here. He wouldn't let them back in the city and wouldn't let them leave the country either. We used to see cars — you know, unmarked? Every few days, out at the main road, they would pass by to spy on us. They were paying the man at the gas station to report on us." She put her hand on my arm and led me away from the house, stepping around a coil of nylon rope in the grass, a capsized stepladder, a roll of chicken wire tied with twine. Here the grass was tufted with native flora and had bare patches where it had been grazed and scratched. "We're running out of money here. Just find El Jabalí, yes? Every Dominican knows him."

"Thank you."

"It's a long way to New York, isn't it?"

"From here? A few hours." The winter afternoons were short. "Irma, I'm so grateful for your time, but really, I have to go. It's a long drive back."

"Yes, of course. You don't want to get stuck out here in the dark."

She walked with me around the side of the house, the veranda curving, stacked with more shrouded furniture. I was looking at my sandals, which were ruined as predicted, when we stepped into the front driveway. The car was gone.

I stood there stupidly for a minute with my mouth open like a fish. "The car is gone," I said.

Irma moved nervously at my side, like a bird rousing. "Gone?" She took a few crunching steps on the gravel.

"He was parked right here." I looked up at the front veranda, and Octavio was standing there, empty-handed, watching me.

"He's gone," he observed.

"Did you see him go?" I said.

"There's a taxi man up the road," Irma said. "We'll send Salvador to get him."

"Can we telephone?" I said.

"No, the telephone doesn't work anymore. No money for the bill."

I let her lead me up the steps. My back was slick with sweat. I pulled the rain jacket off and hung it over the railing as I went up. This was impolite but I was scattered, my thoughts beaming out in every direction like radar. There was something not right about the way Octavio stood there. He appeared to be waiting. Waiting for what? Irma was making soft noises of disapproval about the driver's fecklessness. I followed Irma past Octavio into the front hallway, to a small alcove with a stuffed chair, where she invited me to sit. I stayed on my feet, watching the door. I kept biting my lip, and tried to stop. Irma was ringing an electric bell that sounded somewhere deep in the house, muttering that Salvador never came when he was called, when the front door opened, and the man standing there was not Octavio but a uniformed police officer, and after him another, and another.

The one in front said, "This is her?"

I stepped back. The camera case swung at my side, held shut with its pearl snap; I was outnumbered and not going to use the gun;

they would find it on me. Irma and I stared at each other. She hadn't known.

The policeman in front said, "We've come to talk to you." He was a big man, broad. The two behind him looked younger.

My vision had sharpened. I was watching a movie shot on good film. I was falling backward into a pool. I pretended the camera case meant nothing. I held my purse with both hands instead and one of the younger men stepped forward and pulled it out of my grip. The other snapped to attention, overcame whatever had kept him in the doorway, and gripped my arm, taking the camera case off my shoulder as he did so and dropping a Bakelite bracelet from one of my wrists onto the floor. I thought: If I die here —

Octavio and the big man were conferring in the doorway, and Octavio was pointing away toward the back of the house. "There's a cottage that's empty," he said.

Irma was still staring. She hadn't known and now she was afraid for me. My mouth was dry but I was trying to say something. Finally I did: "I left the jacket on the railing outside." Why that? I wondered where Miguel had gone. Maybe Octavio had sent him away in preparation for calling the police. It was so spiteful of him. He must have been angry that I wouldn't pay them for the house, that I kept insisting on talking to the Ibarras.

"What is this about?" I said, remembering myself. "I haven't done anything."

The big man opened the camera case and held the gun out on the palm of his hand, looking at me with something like pity, as if it were a shame that I was so stupid. "Why do you have this?"

"Wouldn't you?" I said.

They pulled me toward the door.

"I came here alone. I brought it for protection," I said. "I work for a movie studio."

White sunlight fell on us as the door opened. The rain was beginning to clear, clouds scudding away from the invisible sea at the foot of the mountains. I was blinded, and bumped against the policeman who was holding my arm. In the driveway a goat raised its head and fixed me with the blank stare of its alien pupils. They were not taking me to jail. They were taking me instead to the cottage behind the house. Every story I had ever heard about the Dominican police was clattering and heaving in my mind like flotsam from a shipwreck. My knees were shaking, which slowed me down, and the man holding my arm began to pull me along behind him, making impatient noises under his breath. The sun vanished, appeared again. I saw the woman in the solarium again as we went around the outside of the house, looking out over some dead orchids in pots.

Octavio went ahead of us and unlocked the door of the housekeeper's cottage. As if from a distance, I saw the five of us disappear through the doorway into the dim interior.

Chapter 17

The kitchen had a green lino floor, and there was an oilcloth on the table that was printed with blown roses. The counters were bare. Plasticized curtains over the windows made it too dark. The men talked about what to do with me. There were two bedrooms upstairs. Locks on the doors? No, but there were dead bolts in the garage, Octavio could put one on easily. A man would be posted in the house. Who was she?

They turned and looked at me. I was standing in the corner, with fallen plaster from the ceiling crunching under my feet. Octavio switched on the overhead light, which whined and then popped and went out. He grunted and pushed aside the curtains.

"Someone who wants the Ibarras," said the big man. "Bad company." He stepped closer to me. "You're a friend of theirs, that you're looking for them?"

"I work for a movie studio," I said again, knowing that this defense was doomed, that they would want to make calls and corroborate, that the story would fall apart. But it would take a little while.

"That's what these cards say?" said the man with my purse, peering into the case.

"That's what they say," I said.

I remembered being arrested in Baltimore at seventeen, with my mother's car, which she had reported stolen. I remembered the playacting feel of it and the humiliation and how small I felt, how female. The cataract of loss as I sat in the back seat of their cruiser to drive the couple of miles from my aunt's house at the edge of Baltimore to the station house. I could not have been more lost at the bottom of the sea. That was what I imagined Félix Ibarra had felt, waking in the gray morning of Sheepshead Bay. I knew what it was to be sent away.

"My producer's name is Nick Harden," I said. I had seen it on the luggage tags in his room. "He's staying at the Hotel la Colonia."

They chose the upstairs room, the master bedroom. I sat on a stripped mattress and listened to Octavio screw the dead bolt in place on the outside. There was a wicker vanity, host to a crowd of dusty bottles and pots.

The dead bolt was affixed and shot, and I was left alone. I listened to Octavio go back down the stairs to where the policemen waited. I could almost hear what they were saying. I sat on the floor, leaned against the side of the bed. I looked up at the wavering concentric circles that a leak from the roof had left on the ceiling.

The walls were plastered and there were flyspecks around the window. A light fixture in the center of the ceiling had a glass shade, frilled and smoked. A dark mass inside — dead flies. A ceramic lamp on the vanity in the shape of a dancing woman, a painted slipper pointing out beneath a lifted skirt. It was missing its cord. An empty closet. A lightened square on the plaster wall where a chest of drawers had been. A framed print propped against the wall beside the door: *The Virgin of the Rocks,* the paper wrinkled in the frame. The floor was linoleum here too, sprigged with small flowers, a gash in it near the door, as if something heavy had been dragged away. A single window faced the big house. The evening was coming on.

Above the broad tiled roof, glassy streaks of cloud were turning yellow and then orange.

For a long time, no sound from downstairs.

I tried the light switch, but nothing happened. I stood against the wall and watched the room darken. They couldn't have gone far. Maybe they were watching from the windows of the big house. Maybe they were waiting in the yard. When they came back, I did not want to be on the bed.

And then they were back. Footsteps came up the stairs, and then the bolt slid back and two men came in, the big one and another, perhaps a new one. "Come," said the big one, and I didn't move, so he groped in the dark and got my shoulder, and I was pushed through the door and down the stairs, into the blinding light of the kitchen, where the bulb had evidently been changed. A single red chair had been placed at the table.

"Sit down," he said. He looked older in this light: he had taken off his hat and his hair was gray. I looked at the other one, who slumped whenever he stopped moving, a cringing position, a C shape always opening toward the chief.

"Are you deaf?" said the chief, so I sat down.

"What did you come here for?" he said.

"I work for a movie studio," I said. "I go out to find locations to shoot."

"No one believes you."

"Call the man I told you about," I said, but it came out more quietly than I had intended. I couldn't look straight at anything. My mouth was dry.

"We've sent a man to call. We'll see what he has to say when he gets back. Where did you come from?"

"From California."

"But you're Dominican."

"I'm not Dominican."

"You are Dominican."

I hadn't expected that. I looked from one of them to the other. "My cards are in the bag you took. I'm American."

"How long have you lived in the States?"

"Always. I was born in Washington, DC."

I tried to focus on his face but the light was just behind him.

"Who is your family? Who sent you?" he said.

"Nobody sent me, and my family is my mother, and I promise you, she is not Dominican."

"They let too many people out, that's the

problem," the chief said to the other one, who I decided was a deputy, and the deputy nodded. "They let them run to Miami and then they just come back."

"You can hear my accent," I said. "I learned Spanish in school."

"So did my nephews in New Jersey," said the chief.

"I don't know how to tell you —"

"Stop," he said. "I'm bored with that." He stepped forward and kicked the legs out from under the chair. The back of my head bounced on the linoleum and the air left my lungs in a huff of pain. I was dazzled by the overhead light. The hem of my dress had come up. The chief and the deputy stood quietly looking down at me, as if at a gravesite. I took a noisy breath, struggling to sit up. I could not control my face.

"Take her back upstairs," said the chief.

Back upstairs I sat on the bed and shook for a long time. A pain started, a hot throb where my head had hit the floor. My whole body oscillated in the dark like a guitar string. There was no way to mark the time. Eventually I thought: I have to pee. Other demands of the body arose, more faintly than the first. I was hungry and thirsty.

I could die here.

I have to pee.

The two thoughts circled, as if answering each other. The shaking had stopped. I thought, If I pee on the mattress, they might not notice. If I go on the linoleum, it will sit there in a puddle and stink and I think they might kill me for the inconvenience.

But there was a little light around this problem, as if someone had turned on a lamp on the other side of a door. Because it was a demand. I was suddenly possessed of a demand and it couldn't be helped and they would have to respond. I rapped on the door with both hands and shouted, "I HAVE TO PEE."

Footsteps back up the stairs, right away.

"The fuck are you yelling for?" said the deputy. The sound of his voice made the back of my head throb harder.

"I have to use the bathroom," I said.

He said nothing. I pictured him hesitating halfway up the stairs. I wondered if the water was still on in this cottage. Maybe they would have to take me outside, or into the big house. "I can't hold it," I called. "I need water, too, please. I'm so thirsty."

"I don't know," he said, not quite to me.

I shuffled my feet on the floor. "I don't want to make a mess."

The footsteps moved closer. I guessed the chief had gone somewhere else, or he would have been consulted. I could feel the crackle of the younger man's anxiety in the unlit hallway.

"All right," he said, opening the door. My eyes had adjusted to the dark of the bedroom, and I could make out his round face. "Come," he said.

We passed the empty kitchen downstairs and stepped outside. The moon was rising over the big house. Frogs sang in the woods. The dark was manifold, populated. I felt that we were being observed from everywhere by a night full of animals. The other young policeman from before was out there, smoking a cigarette.

"She has to take a piss," said the deputy.

The other man laughed unpleasantly. "There's no line," he said, indicating the broad slope of the lawn in front of us.

My officer took this up, glad to have some suggestion of what to do. "Make yourself comfortable," he said, smirking.

"I can't go behind the house?"

"No. Don't be smart."

I wondered what he thought I would do if I got back there behind the cottage. It was darker and more hidden on the uphill side, but there was nowhere to run except into the forest. I shifted, uncomfortable.

"Is the water running in the big house?"

"Quiet. Go quickly or I'll take you back inside now."

I took a few steps away from him, toward the hedge of overgrown topiary along the back end of the dry swimming pool. "I'm going to go over here."

"Fine."

I crouched in the shadow of the bushes. The ground was soft and muddy under my heels, and a homey smell of rotten leaves rose up. The relief made me feel faint. I looked up: the sky was heavy with stars. There were tears in my eyes. The two men were talking. I felt a hard emptiness, as if I were the husk of a cicada. It was hunger and fear but it felt like my vital parts had left the rest of me behind on this mountain. I was a chitinous shell with large, blank eyes. I stood up, adjusted my clothes, ran my hands through the wet grass. I walked back toward the two men.

"All right," I said.

"Back in," he said.

I didn't know whether to hope that they had really called Nick or not. I ran through every scenario, a wealth of imaginary newsreel, sitting on the edge of the bed because I was afraid there might be palmetto bugs abroad on the floor. Nick is at the hotel and comes down when the desk calls him. Nick is not at the hotel. Nick cannot be found. Nick misunderstands the questions put to him and claims no knowledge of me. Nick assents that he knows me, sure, she's a solo tourist who's been lying next to the pool at a bargain hotel for days. What movie studio? Nick guesses the answers the chief wants to hear and provides them. Nick guesses the answers that I would want him to give, and gives them. My movie studio, my movie. Every one of these scenes stumbled on one point or another. Deep red spots swam in front of my eyes in the dark. I lay down slowly. I was so tired, but my brain glared and revolved like a lighthouse. The mattress exhaled the smell of mildew. I looked up into the almost perfect black of the ceiling. The moonlight at the window did little but make the shadows deeper.

Better to hope that they hadn't called him yet. But if they hadn't, they would in the morning. It was clear already what story was forming in their minds. They thought I was from some exiled dissident family. They thought I was a subversive, or a saboteur. A favorite enemy.

I swam up out of the dark, went to the window, unhooked the casements, pulled them open. A seal of paint broke open. The night was a presence in the room immediately, a smell of flowers. Mosquitoes would come in, but I didn't care. Below me on the lawn, there was a square of light thrown from the kitchen window, where the officer kept watch. Back to the bed again, weaving on my feet from getting up too quickly. It had been so many hours since I had eaten.

Hunger made my brain into a pressurized, gaseous space. The moon had risen high, and the objects in the room suggested themselves in the dark. They were harder to make out when I looked at them straight on. In my peripheral vision they solidified, then melted as I turned my head.

A headache from thirst. Swollen hands from the heat.

Fortress Ozama, standing at the mouth of the river. Galíndez was already dead at some country estate, but they had taken the American pilot who had flown the plane to the prison fort. Kept him alive for a while. A few days? It had been in the paper, years later, in New York.

The plaster for the walls was mixed with the blood of cattle. The blood of goats or pigs. I had owned a book about Ferdinand and Isabella. Ozama, a yellow Spanish fortress on the Dominican shore, where the river flowed into the sea. The walls were six feet thick, blackbirds roosted in holes, at noon the skies darkened like they did over Golgotha.

They didn't shoot the pilot. They strangled him with a rope. He was twenty-three and came from Oregon.

A great looking-glass . . . repeated the vacant majesty of the bed and room. . . . I grew by degrees cold as a stone, and then my courage sank. In the red room, with the light moving on the wall.

My mother, putting her earrings on in the front hallway. The old cat we'd had, gone now ten years. I used to wake up and find him sleeping in the crook of my arm.

A fluttering apology: I didn't mean to. I was stupid, and got lost.

Build it up with silver and gold — silver and gold will be stolen away — stolen away —
Set a man to watch all night.
Suppose the man should fall asleep?

CHAPTER 18

I must have slept, because some time later I was awake and headlights were moving across the ceiling of the cottage. The beams slid from the open and empty closet to the corner above my head and stopped there. The calling of frogs and insects rose to a higher pitch, as if they were offended by the intrusion. My throat was dry, my skin damp and hot, and it took me a moment to catch my breath. In the kitchen below, I heard a cough, a brief conference, and then the front door opening.

I sat up and looked at the pool of light on the wall and ceiling above me. I crossed to the window. Just there, where the driveway curved uphill on its approach to the front of the big house, a car sat idling. I couldn't see anything of it past the glare of the head-lights, attended by flitting moths. The car door opened and shut and a figure moved across the grass.

Another policeman, I thought. Then: He left it running.

The two officers who had been keeping watch in the kitchen emerged now on the lawn below, yelling, "Párese ahí!" The new man, a little way out of the pool of light he had created, raised his hands halfway and called back in gringo Spanish. It was Nick. I dropped below the window sash, rocked back on my heels, rubbed my face, muttered something to myself that turned out to be a solemn thanks to Jesus Christ, tried to get enough air in my lungs. My heartbeat was slippery and violent in my chest. I could hear their voices, threading up through the night, but couldn't catch the words. Nick walked toward the police and the three of them turned and came back toward the cottage.

It was apparent to me what I had to do, and it was terrible. I expanded with it, like a hot-air balloon. I missed my little gun. I rubbed the mosquito bites on my feet and checked the buckles on my useless sandals. The door opened below and the three voices came up through the floor. A chair scraped on the linoleum in the kitchen.

"She's here?" Nick said in Spanish, each vowel round and distinct, as if he were practicing for an oral exam.

261

Some kind of assent.

"But why?" Nick said. "She meant to come straight back."

From the chief: "Why are *you* here?"

"Because I received your telephone message at the hotel."

"It's a long way to drive at night."

"Well, when the police call, you come." His tone shifting, trying to lighten. "Don't you?"

I stood looking down at the grass below the window. It was probably only ten feet, twelve from the lip of the windowsill, but it looked much farther.

The car idled, orbited by its moths. I thought I saw a movement by the house, wondered if someone had come out to see what the noise was about; but no, it was a shadow. My head and back ached from being thrown on the floor. He could explain himself. It probably wouldn't be the first time. He would know what to do.

I had risen up on my toes. I was wasting time, as if I could ease into what I was about to do. An immense darkness rested behind me, lapping at the edges of my vision, and I looked straight ahead.

I pushed the casements open, climbed onto the sill, gripped the frame above me for an instant with both hands, and dropped. The air lifted my clothes and hair and the earth knocked my legs out from under me, a tremendous blow to my feet and knees and then my shoulder and the side of my face. I had never learned the right way to fall. The grass was wet and the pain in my head snapped open like a parachute. I jumped up and ran, my feet slippery in the sandals, past the car Nick had driven, which was pouring the heat of its engine into the sticky atmosphere of the driveway, to the police sedan parked twenty feet away.

I crouched beside the police car and scrabbled at the dust cap on the front tire valve. It was a nightmare, working with these tiny pieces in the dark, my hands shaking. I dropped the cap in the gravel but found it again, pried it apart with my thumbnail, trying to keep my breath from rattling my whole body, and loosened the valve. I heard the hiss of air and pitched the cap into the dark behind me.

What would they do to him?

I ran back across the gravel and got into the other car, knowing that the sound of the door shutting would bring them all out of the cottage, shutting it anyway, feeling for the pedals with both feet, wishing I were barefoot, putting the clutch in and finding reverse, the smooth sweep of a three-point turn, the avenue of mahogany trees rising up before me. The cottage door slammed and the policemen's voices rose in the night. I put the car in first and then second so quickly that it whined at the edge of stalling. A dog ran out of the dark, jubilant, and circled the car. The clutch slipped and caught and I lurched forward, gassed it, hoped desperately that the dog would stay out of the way, and went for third. I could feel the tinniness of the engine. It was a small car, a box, a shell. I heard the police car roar to life behind me and looked in the rearview, but saw only a chaos of lights. The gravel of the driveway turned to the smooth asphalt of the road. The radium glow of the speedometer read fifty kilometers per hour, then sixty, then seventy. The trees rushing past in formation made it seem faster. At a bend, the baleful horse of the Ibarra estate looked out at me from the colonnade of trunks, its huge liquid eyes gleaming yellow-green.

The police car was gaining on me. I shifted into fourth, gave it more gas, and felt the weak striving of the engine. Low-hanging branches flickered in the headlights, bursting forth like pheasants, and made me flinch. The road was narrow and my feel for the pedals was impeded by the stiff and slippery surface of my shoes. The police car surged up, nearly clipping my bumper; I could see that they wanted to pass me and then cut me off, and that the only thing stopping them for now was the close ranks of the mahogany trees, which would give out as soon as this avenue ended at an ordinary road. I shifted to fifth gear. The needle topped out, straining, at 110 kilometers per hour, not much faster than I would have driven on the West Side Elevated at home. The wind in the open window battered me, threw my hair before my eyes. I wished I'd had time to get my seat belt on. There was a bang, and I pitched forward instinctively, hiding my face against the steering wheel. A gunshot or just a piece of gravel flung up by the tires? The car wobbled and I lifted my head again, correcting.

We were by now a mile from the house. There was another bang — I was certain now that they were shooting. I tried to keep the wheels straight. I was all cold, from the crown of my head to my wet feet. The avenue ended, the ranks of trees disappeared, and we streamed into a larger, more airy night. I turned left onto the main road, and the police car followed and jumped forward again, went into the other lane, gaining on me, their front fender to my rear one. I could see their faces in the side mirror; they were shouting. There were three of them. They had all come after me. Their car began to pitch and reel.

I saw it in the mirror, then risked a look back. The police car was weaving, and I saw panic in the face of the deputy at the wheel. The car slowed, then rolled into the right lane and kept going, wobbling, off the road and into the edge of a field, where it stopped. The tire had at last gone flat.

I felt what the old saints must have felt in the face of an unlikely exercise of divine will. I could have floated; I could have taken the battered car up with me. I was weeping. Time compressed into a wild slurry; only a few seconds had passed. And then, still on fire with my luck, I found that I was turning the car around.

I observed this as if from above, with regret. I made a U-turn across the highway with one wheel on the shoulder at the edge of the field, drove the hundred yards back past the police car, ducked below the window for an instant as the men exploded out of their listing vehicle, either saw or imagined the flash of orange as one of them fired at me. There was a reverberating *plink* that I felt through the pedals; they had hit the flank of the car. I sat up and watched them shrink in the mirror. I turned back into the Avenida de las Caobas.

The trees flashed past again. The horse was gone. The road rose up before me, a confusing echo of my arrival there the day before in the back seat of Miguel's car, all the landmarks invisible in the dark, only this tunnel of trunks. I came out from the avenue again and into the circular drive.

I stepped out of the car, leaving it running, not shutting the door. My whole body was shaking, and I wasn't sure if I could stand without one arm on the roof. "Nick!" I called.

An incomprehensible quiet reigned; there was only the sound of the breeze in the forest. Even the frogs had stopped calling. I turned in a circle, unwilling to leave the car. "Nick!" I yelled again.

There were running footsteps, and then there he was, blinking in the headlights, hair wild, eyes round. "What are — what are you —"

"Get in the car!"

He ran for the passenger side and pulled the door shut behind him. I got back in and again put the car in reverse, taking an extra moment to fasten my seat belt. This time, instead of entering the avenue, I turned left onto the dirt farm track that bisected the field, praying that it had an outlet some-where. Leaves slapped the sides of the car, a continual hissing assault. The track dipped over a hill and widened. The lights of a small house in a pocket of the slope appeared and disappeared. The Ibarra house was gone behind us, as if the mountain had closed over it.

"Who *are* you?" Nick said.

"Nobody," I said.

"You left me that note — saying if you weren't back . . . and then the phone call . . ."

The dirt track opened onto a proper road. I let the car idle at the intersection for a moment, and then chose a direction at random. Away, just away. Putting miles behind us.

"I'm a private investigator," I said.

"Oh, come on now."

"It's true. I got into some trouble."

"I can see that."

"I'm looking for a family. That was their place. It's a long story."

Occasionally another car passed us now, and I flinched each time. I kept hearing distant sirens in the whine of the engine.

"I didn't think you were coming back," Nick said. Then, considering: "Maybe you didn't think you were either."

268

"I didn't think anything," I said shortly. "I wish I knew where this road was going."

"I'm not choosey."

"What time is it?" I said.

"It's five. It took me half the night to find a car. I gave fifty dollars to someone for this one — the chambermaid's boyfriend's brother-in-law?"

"I'll pay you back."

He burst out laughing. It went on for a while. "You'll pay me back?" he said. He lit a cigarette.

A man in a gas station on a two-lane road, as the birds were beginning to make their uproar in the trees and the sky was going pale, pointed us the way back to the capital. We had wandered north and would be coming down to it over the hills. I wanted to fill the tank but had no money. I did ask him for a cup of water, which he gave me. My purse was on the mountain and the rest of my money was in the hotel safe. I didn't want to ask Nick for anything else. In the growing light I could see that the bullet had made a neat hole in the front left fender.

"Would fifty dollars fix that?" I said.

"Fifty dollars was just to take it," Nick said. He directed his comments at a white-washed school across the road, a single yellow light over the door.

I walked stiffly; my neck and back had gone tight. I made a circuit of the car.

"We'd better hurry, don't you think?" Nick said, still talking to the school.

"My return ticket is at the hotel," I said. "I can cash it in at the airport and take whatever flight comes first. Do you have money for your return flight?"

He glanced over. Maybe it hadn't occurred to him before this moment that his stay in the Dominican Republic was over. But he took it in. "I have traveler's checks."

"Good."

I saw him looking at the bullet hole before he got back in the car. "I heard the shots," he said.

We pulled back onto the road. I wanted to see the ocean. I felt myself missing something, misunderstanding something, and being accused of it, in the dense silence coming from the passenger side of the car.

A woman I had never seen before was at the front desk of the hotel. We told her we were checking out. I had tried to compose my face and hair in the mirror in the car, but I could tell there was something unraveled about me. Nick was very pale. But she was a hotel night clerk and was used to

270

these things. She paid us no attention.

Nick wrote a message to the chamber-maid, and I put a twenty-dollar bill in the envelope for the damage to the car. It would have been fair to leave more, but I knew I would have to add cash to the value of my ticket to leave that day and my reserves were dwindling. The note said that we were sorry for the inconvenience but had been forced to leave the car in the airport parking lot rather than at the hotel. Nick had adopted an attitude of seamless politeness toward me, as if I were someone's elderly visiting relative. I packed in five minutes, then took another five to panic, thinking I had lost my passport, but it was in a hidden pocket of my suitcase where I had left it. I found Nick waiting for me in the lobby with his bag.

"Christ, I thought you had left," he said, which struck me as funny.

"Again?" I said.

CHAPTER 19

The first American flight was a nine thirty
to Miami, with a connection to New York
two hours after landing. I had just enough
money left for a meal, maybe two. Nick
booked the same flight. We asked to board
early and sat in our separate seats, smoking,
while passengers trickled on.

Some final tension in my chest dissolved
when I could see the ocean below. I fell
asleep and woke to hear the captain's voice
crackling out, "Bienvenidos a los Estados
Unidos," a sentence that sounded to me,
still only half-conscious, like a song.

I found Nick reading the *Miami Herald* and
eating a burger at an unfamiliar fast-food
joint in the Miami terminal.

"Listen," I said. I was standing on the
outside of a railing that separated the premises of the burger stand from the slick and
echoing corridor of the terminal. He low-

ered the paper.

"Listen," I said again, my face flaming.

He stared.

"You're right," I said. "I wasn't going to come back at first. I couldn't see a way to do it. But then I did. I did come back."

A teenage waitress passed, eyeing me.

"And I will give you the fifty dollars," I said. "But I know it's not the same as paying you back."

He chewed on the inside of his cheek. "Why should I be angry, at the end of the day?" he said. "I don't even know you."

"Well," I said. "I guess that's true." I stood there thinking, We could be friends. We are friends, I think. Or we were. But I wasn't the kind of person who could say things like that. Instead I said, "Give me your address, so I can send you a check."

My own street and my own house, cold as a crypt. I goosed the boiler and fell asleep, too tired to take off my stockings, and woke in the dark hours later, the clock showing seven PM. Fatigue had spread over me and my world like tar. I could hardly imagine getting up, and yet felt that I lay in a pit I had to escape. In the dark room, the smells and sounds of the cottage in San Cristóbal rose up — mildew, damp earth, the hissing of insects from the woods. I sat up and turned on all the lights. Then I took a shower, changed into warmer clothes, heated and ate a can of soup in the kitchen without sitting down, and went to the Bracken.

She wasn't there. I hesitated in the doorway, thinking I might see her come out of the kitchen, but Lois, the backup girl who worked weekends, was there instead, picking her teeth in the corner by the till. A couple of braying girls came in behind me, dislodging me from the door, and I tried to shake off my disappointment. There was something spongy and weak about me just then. I could feel it and I hated it. I went to the bar and ordered a whiskey from Lois, and when she brought it to me I said, using a bright and unnatural voice that I had never heard before, "Where's Max?"

"Some girl took her to Key West for the week," Lois said.

I tried to think of something to say while this information screeched past. I had once had a friend whose third-story apartment was next to the elevated tracks of the J train where they rose and rounded a turn in Brooklyn, and each time the train shuddered and hollered by her windows I would feel completely emptied of words, as I did now, while my friend kept chatting, stirring coffee, picking out records for the hi-fi. "Nice time of year for it," I said finally, and thought I saw a smirk on Lois's face. I emptied my drink and asked for another. Peach came in, mercifully, and I talked to her for a while. She was a good soul and you could be a mess with her, and she wouldn't even notice, let alone hold it against you. I told her I had been on vacation in the Caribbean. She professed to be jealous. She had been cleaning out the freezing attic of an aunt who had just died. Out of sympathy, I ordered whiskeys for us both.

At ten o'clock Peach said she had to go home, she was exhausted, and I was alone again at the bar, which by then was gently moving in and out of focus, my glass sometimes becoming two glasses. "Lois, give me a dime for the phone," I said.

"Aw, Vera," she said.

"Come on, Lois. After all the good times we've had?"

She dug in her pocket. I went out to the phone in the vestibule and stood leaning my head against its frigid stainless-steel face for a minute, trying to ward off the spins. I had dialed the number before I knew what I was doing, or that's what I told myself. Jane answered on the third ring.

"Dabrowski residence," she said.

"Hello, Jane," I said.

A pause and then her old outpouring of warmth. "Sweetie, hello. Where are you?"

"At the bar."

"Ah. By yourself?"

"Let me keep some secrets, Jane."

"What else did I ever do?"

Why did the first touch of familiarity feel like this, no matter what had happened, no matter what it meant? She was teasing me. I sagged into the corner, sat on the tiny bench that had been nailed there for that purpose. "I've been traveling," I said thickly. "I was in the Dominican Republic." Then, firmly: "On vacation."

"What a life you lead. I wish I could see you. What bar?"

"The Bracken."

"That's a long way from here." She rented a place by the college.

"Not so long."

"You know, Vera, I've been meaning to call you — I did call you a couple of days ago, actually, but you were away."

"I was away," I agreed. A group of men and women pushed past me, bringing a blast of cold air, and I reeled back into the corner, outraged.

"I just — well, I told you that in the midst

of my — the stupid thing that I did, that she — the woman I was seeing, she took a lot of money from me. And I've been having trouble catching up on my rent."

A word issued from me, a distant "Oh."

"It's not so far to your place," she said, as if this had just occurred to her. "I could come and meet you there."

"You could come and meet me," I repeated.

"Yes. In an hour? I just have to get myself together."

"You know, Jane," I said, very slowly, "I think I'd rather be alone."

All weekend, I had nightmares about the Avenida de las Caobas, the radium eyes of the horse among the dark trees. I sat up late watching television, avoiding sleep. A local station syndicated Johnny Carson episodes on a three-day lag, and I watched Flip Wilson clap politely for the José Molina Dancers. I was drinking, eating poorly, carrying around a perpetual headache, dragging the newspaper off the stoop in the morning. I had planned to mail a check to Nick, but by the time Monday came to deliver me from the desolation of the weekend, I needed to get out of the house. I was worn out from the bitter circle of my thoughts about Max and her girl in Florida, and the damp squib that was left where my anger at Jane had been. I would hand deliver Nick's check. I had his address, after all, and I figured a reporter might be home on a weekday morning.

He lived in a fourth-floor walk-up over a storefront dance studio on East Twelfth Street. I bought some doughnuts at a shop on the corner: another peace offering. The street door to his building was unlocked, and it was quiet as I went up. I knocked on the door of 4B and waited in the carpeted hall, where overcast daylight filtered down from a skylight. It was beginning to snow.

I heard footsteps, and then the hesitation of a look through the peephole. The door opened. "This is a surprise," he said, not unkindly.

"I brought your money," I said. "And —" I held out the greasy bag, and he took it. I watched him think over his options while he held it.

"Well, come in," he said after a moment.

The apartment was small, tidy, a bit spartan. There were a couple of austere line drawings on the living room wall. He went into the kitchen and came back with a coffee pot.

"I wasn't sure I'd be welcome," I said.

He shrugged. "Sit down," he said. "Is it snowing?" The patch of sky through the living room window had gone soft and gray. I sat at a table and laid the check down in front of me. He folded it and put it in his pocket. He looked like he had made up his mind about something. He pivoted toward me.

"I have questions," he said.

"Questions?"

He set a teacup painted with roses in front of me and filled it with black coffee. "Questions about you."

"Oh. Well. All right —"

"Are you in the CIA?"

"People keep asking me that," I said to the teacup.

"Was that why you were so angry at the club? Because you were running your operation and I was trying to run mine —"

"You were running an operation?"

"Figuratively, figuratively."

Intelligence and journalism weren't so far apart. It was always the sources who mattered. Both disciplines were a mass of deflecting and waiting and preparing. "I guess so," I said. "I was angry about getting caught up in something without being told first. It's dangerous to be around an intelligence officer, you know, if your intentions

279

are — informational."

"Informational!" He sat down in the other chair and emptied the doughnuts onto a plate.

"I'm not in the CIA," I said.

"Well, that's what you would say, isn't it?" I could tell that he was both joking and not joking at once. A pigeon on the ledge outside the window complained moodily about the snow. What kind of secrets was I supposed to keep now? I worked for myself, after all, didn't I? What did I have to tell at this moment that could really do me any harm?

"I used to work for the CIA," I said. "I quit a year ago."

"They hire women?" Surprise on his face.

"Sometimes. People don't expect us, so much."

"They hire queers?"

I laughed. "Of course not."

"Is that why they fired you?"

"They didn't fire me, I quit. I did an operation in Argentina and got stranded, and they left me there."

His eyebrows went up. "Argentina, last year? The coup?"

"In '66, yeah. I was there doing surveillance. But then Onganía came in and they shut down the ports and I was stuck for a long time. After I finally got out —" Again I saw the inside of the Britten Norman airplane banking low over the Falkland Islands, the soccer field tilting wildly into view. "I got out on my own, came back here to New York, and quit."

"They let you go?"

"I wasn't so valuable."

"And now you're a private eye."

"Well, that sounds kind of silly. An investigator, yes."

"What were you doing in the Dominican Republic?"

"I can't talk about that."

"Sure you can."

I turned the spoon around in my cup. "Look, have you ever heard of a Dominican exile named El Jabalí?"

He crossed his arms. "I can't believe this."

"What?"

"You really are an investigator. I'm sitting here in my apartment with a lady private eye."

I disliked that.

"You don't like that at all," he said.

I tried to make my face more neutral. "Have you heard of him?"

"Yeah. He's big time."

"Well," I said. "This big-time guy, if you were looking for him, where would you go?"

He thought it over. "I'd go up to the social clubs in Washington Heights. There are a lot of Dominican clubs up there now."

"Members only?"

"No, you can pay fifty cents at the door and they'll let you in. That's where all the exiles hang out."

I could make inquiries. There were a couple of Dominican girls I drank with the in Village sometimes. Maybe they could direct me. "Let's say you're Balaguer," I said. I had a question I had been turning over in my mind.

He laughed. "Let's say."

"Let's say you have a political enemy. People like him, they want him to run for president against you. He leaves the island and runs to New York."

"All right."

"Do you go after him?"

He thought about it. "Only if I'm really afraid of him."

"But why? What can he do from New York?"

He laughed. "You said it yourself."

"I did?"

"He can get to El Jabalí! He's the power center of the Dominican exile. He's connected on the island, in New York, *and* in Washington. His real name is Rosales, I think. Or Rosas? Something like that. He made his money in textiles. He had legitimacy."

"He did?" I said. "What happened?"

"Trujillo pushed him out. Balaguer would worry about an enemy who wants to run for president and who reaches El Jabalí. I mean, think about the invasion in '65. Think about the Bay of Pigs! The CIA can be very fickle in their affections. They're with Balaguer now, but what if they had an alternative? If I'm Balaguer, I'm worried that if El Jabalí starts talking to his Washington contacts about my enemy and how popular he is on the island, the CIA will pick a new horse. People don't love Balaguer and he knows it, the CIA knows it. What happened when the CIA stopped loving Trujillo? He was dead on the road out of Santo Domingo."

"It was his own people who did that."

"But they wouldn't have done it if the CIA was still with him. The wind had changed."

The pigeon at the window took wing and disappeared. There are some enemies you exile and some you keep close. Balaguer's people had come for the boy because they knew his parents had come for him too. They must have been reading their letters, or paying off their staff. I thought of Octavio. When the Ibarras left the island, it would have been easy to guess they would come here.

"Why did the police pick you up?" Nick said.

I huffed. "One of the servants gave me up. He must have thought the police would be pleased with him. They all thought I was a spy." I stared out the window at the side of the next building. The bricks at the top of the wall each had their own edge of clinging snow. "He must have sent my driver away. It was stupid of me to go there alone. To go there at all." I had wanted to matter, I thought. That was the idiot root of the whole thing.

"Why'd you come when they called you?" I said.

"Well, you had left me that note."

"Sure. But why did you come?"

He tilted his head. "Would you have come?"

I thought about it. "You had only just met me."

"Would you have come, though?"

I imagined receiving a note like the one I had written. *If I'm not back —*

"You must have thought I would come," he said. "Or you wouldn't have left it."

"Maybe I left it because I didn't have any

better ideas," I said.

"You haven't answered my question."

"It doesn't usually pay, does it? Hoping someone will show up."

"Is that what you've found?"

"That's a different question." I lifted the coffee cup, but it was empty. I pretended to drink from it anyway. Why?

"I just wanted to know," he said. "Because it's one of the more interesting things that's ever happened to me, to be honest. I've been chewing it over."

"Would a normal person have gone?" I said.

"Is neither of us normal?"

"The thing is," I said, "I think a normal person *would* have gone."

"But you just said it doesn't usually pay."

"Well — among people I've known, I guess."

"Have they not been normal either?" he said.

I tried a joke. "It's every man for himself around here."

"I think you like to think you're on your own and it's a cold world, et cetera, et cetera," he said. "It excuses some things."

I could feel my face flush red. "Excuses what kind of things?"

"Being cold."

I blinked. "You don't know a thing about my life."

"Every queer in New York has a sad story. Everyone's been thrown away once or twice." He looked placid. He leaned forward, saw my cup was empty, and filled it again.

"Thrown away," I said.

"Sure. Family, friends, lovers. If you make it to thirty without having your heart broken a few times —"

"I haven't made it to thirty yet."

He laughed. "I hate to tell you, but I think you will. So you might want to make some friends."

■ ■ ■ ■

IV
MARCH 1968

NEW YORK

■ ■ ■ ■

CHAPTER 20

Félix had been cut early for the night. The boss came and let him go at eight because the weather was so bad; sleet was nearly horizontal down the street in front and only two parties had been seated since seven. Félix had tried to argue because he wanted to stay long enough for his shift meal, but he couldn't find the words to make his case. Sergei, the Russian cook, must have guessed, because he handed Félix a burger, made quickly at the back of the grill from the last bits of the lunch special, boxed up in waxed cardboard, with mashed potatoes scooped from the pot. Sergei hardly talked to anyone, but he always shared cigarettes and he was the best whistler in the kitchen, and if you guessed what song he was whistling, he would give you a nickel.

So Félix walked home at 8:15, gloveless, holding the box in front of him, warming his hands on it. No cars passed; only a bus, crawling at half speed. Some storefronts had low lights in them, but many were dark. He passed the jewelry store, where he always noticed the empty stands for necklaces and rings and the perforated cards for earrings, all of it stripped at closing time. In the late mornings, on his way into work, diamonds glittered there, and rubies, a shocking pink. In the window of a hardware store, work lights on clamps beamed down on a pyramid of silver paint cans.

Félix turned right, into the narrow dark street that led to the house. He was thinking that if he could fall asleep early then he wouldn't mind the quiet of the house so much.

It was a steep climb and it warmed him up. When the house came into view, he saw that a few windows were lit; he began to hope that some other boys might be playing cards. Maybe they had also come home early. Some of them worked at another restaurant a few blocks away and were probably having the same kind of night he was.

His fingers were numb, and it was while he was fumbling with the door on the front porch that he heard the noise out of the darkness, the inquiring high note, and then felt the bump against his leg.

"Rubén?" he said, and again the bump, again the soft question.

The cat slept in Félix's bed that night, and in the morning he left the animal curled on the fretful lump of Carmelo, who was sick and would probably not move from in front of the gas heater all day. Félix tore a stick of beef jerky into pieces and left it there for Rubén. He kept putting his hand on the cat's head, his mysterious ears; he was so soft. Félix was late leaving for work and almost ran the last two blocks. The streets were blinding, every roof and twig coated in dripping ice. In his hurry to reach the door of the restaurant before his pay could be docked, he didn't notice the woman in the blue coat sitting on the bench in front of the hardware store, smoking, or see her lift a camera and point its telescoping lens at him.

I was almost certain that it was him. I had spent the past four weeks up and down the Hudson Valley, calling every restaurant on the bus line that Félix had taken, asking for Bobby Candelario, giving his description, and had already spent a cold day waiting outside a steak house in Valhalla where the manager had said they had a Bobby but couldn't say what his last name was. That Bobby, when I'd finally gotten a look at him, had been at least five years too old. But this Bobby in Peekskill was young, slight, and bore a resemblance to the photograph in the Saint Jerome file. The manager had called him Bobby Calendario, had said that his English wasn't good. I took three pictures of the boy approaching, crossing the street in a rush against the light, pulling off his hat as he reached for the door of the restaurant. He had no gloves on. His coat was too big for him and he hadn't bothered to button it; was it one of the hated green church coats the Saint Jerome boys wore? The glaring sunlight made it hard to tell the color. He disappeared through the brass front door of La Cucina, and I dropped my cigarette and walked back to my car. My toes had gone numb during the hour I had waited outside the restaurant for the start of the second shift. I was humming, buzzing. The whole day seemed to join me in cracking happily apart.

A second stop, in Oakwood. I parked in a lot near the river, at the end of a hiking trail that was barely marked. I had a map from the Parks Department, and had changed into sturdier shoes. The day had warmed enough to melt most of the ice off the trees, but clouds had rolled in during the afternoon, and the wind off the river chilled the woods. The trail was muddy and took a circuitous path upward, digging into the soft flank of the hill, switchbacking as it rose. I was out of breath climbing it, carrying a heavy rucksack I had brought from the car, and had to unwind my scarf and stop once or twice to rest. The damp in the air smelled like spring, despite the cold.

At the top of the hill, a hutch in a clearing contained a burnt-wood trail map. I took the path that went toward the cliffs, shifting under the weight of the bag. The ground sloped down, the path reinforced with wooden steps made from railroad ties, and then leveled out. The woods were quiet, gray and dun; here and there in the denuded undergrowth I caught glimpses of the surreptitious lives of teenagers, beer cans and candy bar wrappers, scraps of clothing and magazines. In the lee of a downed beech there was a blackened fire pit, filled with ice that had survived the morning.

The cliff came into view abruptly, screened by leafless young maples. I approached cautiously, aware of the slippery ground, feeling that the white sky over the Hudson was suddenly much closer than it had been before. At the edge, bare granite forced a break in the trees, and a view opened up: the immense river, the Palisades on the west side fringed with their own gray lace of woods, the stippled hills rolling southward on the east. I took a rope and my camera from the bag and tied the rope to the strap. The bag was old, and I had put bricks in it, wrapped in newspaper. I was not at all sure that it would achieve the effect I wanted. The muddy ground would help. Where it sloped away from my feet, I tied one end of the rope to a tree and pitched the bag forward with both hands. It dragged to a stop before it reached the edge of the cliff, but left a gratifying streak of bare earth through the wet leaves. I hauled it back and threw it again, and this time it went over, the cord snapping taut. I pulled it back up, hand over hand, and then picked my way carefully down the slope and broke off a few saplings, tore up a bittersweet vine. When I stood back, it looked all right. I circled around it, taking pictures with the heavy flash.

"Doesn't it bother you that they're here?" I said. We were in a place Gerry had chosen this time, a bright, buzzing restaurant where they would bring you a slice of cake if you claimed it was your birthday. Plate glass overlooked East Thirty-Third Street. The booths in front were filled with little girls in Sunday outfits.

Gerry shrugged, his most irritating gesture. "All right, I don't like it much."

"What about Galíndez?"

"Nobody was happy about Galíndez."

"There are rules, aren't there?"

He was drinking Earl Grey with milk. It was an awful day, the red lights of the avenue dimmed by freezing rain. He looked up at me. "What kind of question is that?"

"You don't want to know who they are, these people who hired me?"

"Vera, we both know who they are."

"I could get you something — a license plate, maybe. An address, if they're sloppy."

He was tired of this now, scanning the room for the waitress. "What would I do with it?"

"Let your bosses know, get a meritorious write-up, get them sent home."

"Look, Vera, this is how it works," he said. A dessert cart stuck with lit sparklers went by, and a table full of children let out a wail of delight. He leaned over his mug of tea. He looked tired around the eyes. "We go where we want, and we take our army if we feel like it, and they pretend it was their idea. And if they do a good enough job pretending, then they get to go where they want, too, but not in great numbers, and when we see them, we pretend not to."

"That's what intelligence is?"

"That's what an alliance is," he said.

I had been giving Mr. Ibarra bulletins by telephone every two weeks since I returned, telling long-winded stories with just enough progress in them to get to the next call. But now it was finally time to meet. I asked him to come to my office, and the two of them were there in the vestibule that afternoon, the old country doctor and his pin-curled wife.

"Mr. Ibarra," I said, extending a hand.

"Miss Kelly," he said.

"I'm glad you came," I said, ushering them into the office. I waited until they were seated. "I'm sorry to say that I have terrible news."

The wife blinked at me through thick glasses. Mr. Ibarra looked at her uncertainly, and then back at me.

"Your nephew drowned," I said. "I'm so sorry. I just confirmed it yesterday."

I took a malicious enjoyment in watching them struggle to react in the right way. Their surprise was genuine. It could almost have been shock. I switched on a lamp and spread the photographs of the cliffs across the desk, along with a sheaf of papers marked across the top with OAKWOOD POLICE DEPARTMENT. "He was reported missing from foster care on November 9," I said. "There was a search — they kept it very quiet. The police went up to a spot in the woods where the boys from Saint Jerome like to go, and they found this." The photograph of the muddy streak through the leaves at the edge of the cliff, the broken saplings and vines. "The fall is forty feet."

"He fell?" said the wife.

I nodded.

"Did anyone see?" said the husband.

"In the end two boys admitted they were there when it happened," I said. I pushed two typed pages across to him. "Here are their sworn statements."

I watched Mr. Ibarra read. After a long time he said, "He slipped."

"It was raining," I said.

Mrs. Ibarra's face was crumpled in something that looked like confusion. She covered it with her handkerchief, and her shoulders began to shake. I wanted them both to dissolve like tissue paper. I wanted to walk out and close the door and let the whole building sink into Fifteenth Street behind me. And that was almost what was happening. If I concentrated hard enough, it felt like that. I kept my hands folded and watched Mr. Ibarra pretend to comfort his wife.

"Perhaps it would be better if his parents were dead," Mr. Ibarra said suddenly. "Better dead than to hear this news."

Maybe there was real feeling there — real antipathy. Something animating all this. But they were probably only professionals. "Some would say so," I said.

"A nightmare," Mrs. Ibarra said.

"I couldn't give news like this without confirmation," I said. "And I only got the last of the police reports yesterday. They take their time in Oakwood."

"Poor child," Mrs. Ibarra said. Her face was red, but dry.

"Better to remember him as he was," I said.

"Did they find the body?" Mr. Ibarra said.

"No," I said. "The river is very deep."

I smoothed the missing child police report that I had taken from the St. Jerome's file room. The other documents were good matches for it. I had paid my skilled friend in Flushing thirty-five dollars for the whole set. The rubber stamp that said OPD EVIDENCE, which I had applied across the

298

backs of the photographs, had cost me eighty-five cents to have custom-made in a novelty shop on East Ninth Street.

CHAPTER 21

Since I returned from the island, I had been
spending two nights a week uptown, in the
social clubs of Washington Heights, looking
for El Jabalí. It was a helpless kind of orbit,
because I had nothing but the nickname to
go by, and a nickname is an ineffective way
to summon a man who I imagined, like others of his type, did not want to be sum-
moned. Without quite realizing it, I pictured
him as Nico, my contact in Buenos Aires.
They were both men who dispensed and
called in favors, a venerable line of business.

The clubs opened for dancing at night,
but during the day they hosted every kind
of group activity, from table tennis to box-
ing, from dominoes and chess to weight lifting and wrestling. They were huge rooms
that had been put to other uses before the
wave of Dominicans had come to Washington Heights. They had been laundromats
and auditoriums and discount clothing

stores, and the newly arrived had made them over with slogans and banners and patriotic paint schemes. To meet the many social purposes of the clubs, folding tables and chairs were put out, arranged, re-arranged, and folded away each day, like troops of Ziegfeld dancers running through choreography. The tang of the gym, of concrete block and fresh paint and sweat, lingered in the evenings, reminding me of my old high school. I copied the look of the other women, who wore vivid dresses, matching heels, and thick, dark eye makeup. It was usually the old men I asked about El Jabalí, the ones who were already established at a corner table before I came in and hardly left it, except to dance a turn or two with their wives. For weeks I circulated among the clubs, paying the nonmember fee at the door, and no one did more than shake their head in response to my question. I felt conspicuous, but reasoned that if I kept this up, a curious word might reach El Jabalí eventually, of a white girl who was being persistent. On my second or third tour through a club called El Nacional, an old man finally leaned forward and said, in English, "What you want him for?"

"There's a family I need to find," I said. "They left DR looking for their son."

"What's that have to do with him?"

"He helped them," I said, over the bachata coming from the speakers just behind us. "That's what I heard."

He leaned back and glanced at the man next to him — some silent conference. "Haven't seen him," he said.

"Well, thanks anyway," I said.

That was the closest I had gotten, and that was as far as it went. It was a long way home, the rattling A train as far as West Fourth Street, where I sometimes got out and caught a taxi if I was too exhausted to proceed. If I took trains all the way it was an hour and a half in my party dress, reading an Eric Ambler novel to stay awake, creaking into my house at two or three o'clock in the morning with nothing to show but blisters.

Then one evening I was lingering at the serving window of the little kitchen in the back of Club La Patria, chatting with a cook named Pilar while she fried plantains, and she nodded into the milling crowd and said, "There he is."

"There who is?" I said, turning to look.

He was a small man in a pressed yellow shirt, perhaps in his fifties, and I probably wouldn't have noticed him if not for the movement around him: an inner circle of young men standing close, and a larger circle of people passing and offering greetings, or shifting from foot to foot as if preparing to ask a question, or simply slowing to look at him. El Jabalí wore a gray mustache and glasses with thick rims, and his hair was dyed black. I watched while a man approached and leaned in to speak to him. El Jabalí gripped the man's shoulder while he spoke, his face impassive, scanning the room, and then released him with a nod. The man disappeared into the crowd, visibly relieved.

"You were looking for him, weren't you?" Pilar said.

"Yes," I said. "I was starting to think he was a fairy tale."

She laughed. "Oh, he's as real as you and me."

I wondered how I could get close to him. It was like trying to speak to a bride at a wedding, a debutante at a ball. His party ushered him to a table right in front of the bandstand, which was empty that night. The rest of the room was drinking beer and sweet wine out of plastic cups at a quarter apiece, but on El Jabalí's table a bottle of rum appeared with a tray of real glasses. He settled in and lit a cigarette.

"I've got *costillas* in the back for him,"

Pilar said, and hurried away from the window.

A man asked me to dance, and I said all right, and we took a turn or two around the room to the merengue record playing over the PA. While we danced, I saw El Jabalí stand up to talk with an older man, and they walked to the hallway that led out past the kitchen. The song ended and I thanked my dance partner and hurried toward the coat check, which was a card table and a dress rack on wheels, where I had left my purse with a teenage girl chewing gum over a glass jar marked *Propinas.* She gave the bag to me and I searched in it to make sure it still contained the envelope with the photographs of Félix in Peekskill.

El Jabalí was standing at the end of the hall outside the kitchen with the older man, his arms crossed, his gaze on the floor. I didn't know how many chances I might have, and at least at that moment he wasn't surrounded by his younger entourage. I clacked toward them over the tiles, and both looked up at me, irritation quickly hidden under a thin chivalry.

"Miss?" said the older man.

"Sir," I said to El Jabalí. "Could I speak to you privately?"

The older man stepped back, eyebrows

raised, but El Jabalí glanced at him and he stopped where he was. "Regarding what?"

"It's private."

"Are we acquainted, miss?" he said.

"We're not."

"Then I don't think we have anything to talk about."

I had no room to be cautious, then. "I need to speak to Dionisio and Altagracia Ibarra," I said, tense. "They're looking for their son, and I've found him."

The two men stared. I pulled the photographs out of my bag and held them up. "This is him," I said.

They looked at each other. El Jabalí coughed and said, "You have a moment to come upstairs?"

"Yes, okay," I said.

Climbing a staircase again, with parties unknown; but I went. This was a family place. I listened to his footsteps behind me. At the top of the stairs he went around me and switched on a light. We were standing in an office. Deep shelves against the walls held cascading stacks of paper, bound ledgers, and a couple of typewriters, one with the ribbon pulled out. El Jabalí sat in a creaking chair and indicated another one for me. "Let me see those," he said.

I handed him the set of photographs. I

had copies. They were the best that had come from that day, Félix crossing the street in Peekskill against the light, his left profile and then his right as he looked both ways for traffic, the too-big coat flying out behind him as he reached the restaurant door. El Jabalí looked carefully at them, then rested his chin on his fist.

"How do you know this family?" he said.

"It's a long story," I said.

He regarded me. He had a broad, open face, and there was no indication whatsoever of what he was thinking. "Where were these taken?"

I hesitated. "Not far."

"You tell me where, and I tell his parents."

"You know where they are?" I said, deflecting.

He didn't answer, as if it were a rhetorical question. The palms of my hands were beginning to sweat. I opened my mouth to explain that I didn't want to say where he was, that I couldn't hand off this information to a person I had just met, that I had to be able to see for myself that the boy was safe. But I suspected that saying all that would seem like an apology or the opening of a negotiation to someone like him. I closed my mouth again.

"You don't trust me?" he said. "I trust you

even less, don't you think?"

"Sure," I said, shrugging. "That's why you won't tell me where the Ibarras are."

"Of course not." He spread his hands. "So we are stuck, are we not?"

Funny that we had stumbled so quickly into an honest conversation. "We could arrange a meeting," I said.

"Yes?"

"If you tell me a place where the Ibarras will be, I'll bring Félix."

"It would be dangerous for them," he said.

"I'm not a danger."

He turned his hand palm up, as if to show how little it meant for me to say that. He leaned back, and we both sat thinking. Then he said, "They won't come alone. There will be people watching."

I was relieved. "Your people?"

The blank, open face again.

"That's all right," I said. "I accept."

Félix did not usually speak to customers, except to offer to take away empty dishes. Some of the busboys took drink orders and ran plates, but this task was reserved for the ones who had worked at La Cucina longest. Only on the busiest nights did Félix join the fray in the dining room — on New Year's Eve, on Valentine's Day. So it was a surprise

307

when Paulie came back to where he was standing by the Hobart, polishing glasses to prepare for the dinner service that would start in two hours, and said, "A lady out there wants to speak to you."

"To me? Why?"

"She said she knows somebody you know. Hurry up."

It was probably a mistake; no one in Peekskill, outside of the house on the hill, knew anybody he knew. It was a Friday afternoon, and he wondered if she were a truancy officer. He could have gone the other way, walked out the back. But curiosity held him, and a note of pleasure at being looked for. He dried his hands on the front of his apron and pushed through the swinging doors.

It was the dead time of the afternoon, three thirty, and only four tables were occupied in the front room. He saw her immediately, a woman alone at a two-top by the front window, staring out at the street. She had a glass of water and a menu. Her bag and umbrella were hooked over the other chair. He approached around the edge of the room, feeling shy now. She looked younger than he had expected, and had curly hair pinned up, and lipstick on. His stomach turned: she was obviously looking for someone else, and would be disappointed when she saw him.

But she turned and smiled. "Félix."

He panicked, began to back away. "It's Bobby."

"It's all right, Félix," she said. "Believe me."

He was so young. He had, somehow, the same blurriness that the photos had. His eyes were large and dark and he hadn't had a haircut in a long time. His shoes were a mess. I watched him negotiate with himself, standing a good ten feet away from my table, plans going through his head. His name was a password. Probably no one had called him by it in a long time.

"Listen, listen," I said, putting my hand on the other place setting at the table. "Sit down for a minute."

"I can't sit. I'm working." The soft accent. His eyes darted to the side, toward the kitchen.

"Okay, stand closer."

He took a few steps, close enough so I could lower my voice. "Your name is Ibarra," I said. "I'm here to take you to your parents."

It was because he had imagined it a thousand times. The arrival of a stranger with good news, into the everyday mess and slush of his life. Or the arrival of the two of them, the faces that shifted in his memory if he tried too hard to picture them, like numbers in a dream. After Mrs. Villanueva died, he had imagined it all the time. In the intake center, lying in the bunk bed, listening to the roar of the expressway all night, and during his first weeks at Saint Jerome, he would picture them coming for him, his mother with her lily smell, his father with his gold watch, stepping out of a car and saying, "Él viene con nosotros." His father using the voice he used on the telephone in the study, which would neutralize the directors of the intake center, of Saint Jerome, would vaporize them where they stood. "Ustedes no entienden, pues no importa, él viene con nosotros."

Because he was afraid sometimes that he could use up his memories of their faces, that they could fade from his mind like a picture that was handled too much, he had turned more and more to daydreams of an interceding stranger. So that was why, when the woman in the restaurant used his name, his real name, he knew already that he was leaving with her. There was a burst of fear and daylight in his chest. But there was nothing else to do. He went back to the

310

kitchen, found Paulie talking to the chef, said, "I have to go."

"The hell do you mean, you have to go?" the chef said.

"I don't feel good," he said.

"Who was that woman?" Paulie said.

"I have to go," he said, taking off the apron. He was smiling and terrified. Paulie and the chef looked at each other.

"What's the matter with you?" Paulie said, but Félix was already walking away.

El Jabalí had said that Félix's parents would wait for us in Fort Washington Park, in Washington Heights. And if they weren't there, what then — bring him back here? I walked ahead of him out of the restaurant, leading the way to my car. When I glanced back, he was looking at me, and then every-where else, up and down the street. I was trying to think of what to say. All that came out was, "You're all right? You've been okay?" two or three times, while we found the side street where I had parked. He nod-ded (what else could he do?). There were heavy ceramic planters on the sidewalk and electric-green shoots were just appearing in the black dirt inside. "It's almost spring," I said, turning around again, since he was keeping pace two steps behind me, but he didn't answer and I didn't bother to repeat it.

"I like your car," he said softly, when we reached it.

"This?" It listed at the curb.

"Chevy is a good car," he said, and I realized that he was trying to be polite, to make conversation. I was pierced. I opened the driver's side, got in, leaned over to push open the other door. He didn't move. He was skinny and headless through the window, wearing just a T-shirt under his open coat. "Félix?" I said.

"How do you know them?" he said, bending down to look in.

I tried to think how to answer that truthfully, since I didn't actually know them, since every piece of this story was backward. "I found a man who knows them," I said.

"But who are you?"

"I'm a private investigator," I said.

He frowned.

"A detective. Somebody paid me to find you," I said. "I can tell you on the way."

But something about getting into the car, this final commitment, was stopping him. He shook his head. "I have to work," he muttered. "They'll be mad." He shuffled away, looking back the way we'd come.

I was afraid he might run and I wanted to

get out of the car, but I could tell it was moves like that that would make him run. "I'm telling you the truth," I said. "I've been to Hacienda la Romana. I spoke to Octavio and Irma."

And it was back, the flicker of hope that I had seen in the restaurant. He got into the car.

"They are okay?" he said.

"They're fine."

He put on his seat belt. "The radio works?" he said.

It was one of those tentative days at the end of winter, the late afternoon sky pale blue and layered with thin clouds at the horizon. We drove south, Félix playing with the radio buttons, tuning in to distant rock stations, pausing over the salsa music drifting up from the Bronx, shaking his head when the signals weakened and crackled out. I kept the heat on and aimed all the vents at him. I had stopped at a McDonald's on the way out of Peekskill and he sat with the wreckage of the meal in his lap. He had twisted the yellow papers that had been wrapped around the burgers into tight points, had collapsed the cardboard boxes into squares, and then torn off the strips and tabs that held them together. As my car shuddered its way onto the Sprain Brook Parkway he said suddenly, "My cat?"

"You have a cat?"

"Yes," he said. "At the house."

I tried to imagine where he'd been living. "Will it be all right tonight?"

"I think Carmelo will feed him tonight, if he sees I don't come."

"Carmelo?"

"Yes. It's many boys."

"Many boys? Are they all from Saint Jerome?"

"No, they come from other places. They come up to work."

"We'll come back for him," I said. "We'll come back for your cat." And maybe see about all those kids, I thought.

"He likes me the best," Félix said, matter-of-fact. "He'll be lonely."

"Not for long," I said. "I promise."

He grew quiet as Yonkers became the Bronx. We came down from the West Side Elevated into the already shadowed side streets of Upper Manhattan. It occurred to me finally to say, "I'm sorry about Mrs. Villanueva."

He said nothing. I didn't press. I was looking for parking, which was a good excuse. Félix turned the radio up abruptly, a burst of static between the afternoon classical sta-

314

tion and the news. I was startled, annoyed, and then he turned it off. "So who paid you?" Félix said. "My parents paid you?"

"No," I said. "No. What happened was — well." I saw a spot in front of a laundromat and cautiously ratcheted into it. "It was somebody else. They were pretending to be your family."

"Pretending? Why?"

"I think they were looking for your parents, and they were hoping that if they found you, they would find them."

"It was Balaguer?"

"I think it was his people, yes."

I watched his eyes work back and forth. He twisted the papers again.

"They're not looking for you anymore," I said. "I made them think you were dead."

His eyes widened. "Dead?"

"Drowned in the river."

He laughed. "I'm a very good swimmer," he said.

"Glad to hear it."

We seemed to be collaborating, covertly, in delaying our exit from the car.

"My parents are here?" Félix said after a minute.

"In the park," I said.

He leaned forward and put his forehead on the dash. "And if they are not here?" he said to his shoes.

"Well," I said. My eyes stung. "I hope they are."

We crossed Riverside Drive on a footbridge and descended into Fort Washington Park. The trees were still bare, but here and there green things lit up the dark undergrowth. The sun was low now over the Palisades, and we were blinded as we walked downward, along a winding path past tennis courts, into the cold shadow of the George Washington Bridge. It was still too chilly for the park to be busy; the lawns that opened here and there among the trees were empty, with occasional dog walkers and old men. I wrapped my scarf more tightly, and even Félix was moved to button up his coat.

"Where I died," Félix said.

"What?" I said, startled.

"I died there," he said, indicating the river, which lay before us in its most oceanic state, deep blue, white-capped to the shore by the evening wind.

"You certainly did," I said.

He laughed. "I'm a ghost," he said. "I can do anything."

He was walking ahead of me and I wanted to pull him back, slow him down. El Jabalí had told me that the Ibarras would wait for us at the red lighthouse that stood on the rocks at the foot of the titanic bridge. I could see it already, almost orange in the evening light, dwarfed by the immense network of steel girders above it, with a few figures grouped in its small territory: men fishing and couples looking at the view, taking photographs of each other. The wind sliced through my coat.

Félix stopped. I almost bumped into him, then looked to see where he was looking. A couple in dark coats stood at the railing, close together against the wind, facing us. As I watched them, I saw the woman cover her mouth with a gloved hand.

I was warm all at once, flushed, shaking. Félix walked toward them, and they came to meet him. I watched them embrace. His mother was weeping. His father turned away and pulled his glasses off.

I waited a minute, until the three of them broke apart and Altagracia Ibarra turned in my direction. She was small, her hair sharply bobbed under a wool beret. I walked up to her, unsure what to say. There was a great deal but there was also very little. "Hello," I said.

"Who are you?" Altagracia said. "He didn't tell us. Just that he'd seen a photo."

"I'm Vera," I said.

"He told us to be prepared to run," she

said, "in case it was a trap. He told us it was our decision to come or not come."

"El Jabalí did?"

"Yes. And he sent a man with us." She nodded toward the end of the narrow road that led down the hill, where a sedan was idling, a man in it watching us over the top of the *Daily News.*

"He said he would," I said.

"We looked for Félix every day," Dionisio Ibarra interrupted, pressing his fingertips to his eyes. He was tall, wearing a well-made black coat, but with an untidy gray beard beginning across his cheeks. He hugged me, smelling like cigarettes and old coffee. They both looked exhausted.

"They had taken our passports," said Altagracia when Dionisio had let me go.

"I know," I said.

"We couldn't come. But then Esmeralda stopped writing and we had to get papers somehow."

Félix's eyes and nose were red. He stepped away to look over the railing. His father went with him, one hand on his back.

"My husband drove to Sheepshead Bay every day," Altagracia said. "We didn't know what to do. I got the death certificate for Esmeralda but it didn't help. We went to all the hospitals and the medical examiner's office." She squinted at me. "Who are you?" she said again. "Are you with the CIA?"

"No," I said. "Two people came to me last winter and asked me to find your son. They pretended to be your husband's aunt and uncle."

"His aunt and uncle?"

"They said you and your husband were in prison."

She looked shocked. "We thought someone might come after us when we left the Dominican Republic," she said. "But we didn't think they knew about Félix, where we had sent him. They must have been reading our mail. We even had someone else post it for us — but they're everywhere. Spies for Balaguer. Everyone talks." Then she stepped back, her eyes narrowing. "Where are they now, these people who lied to you?"

"I told them he was dead. I showed them some fake records. They won't bother you. It's a long story."

"Why did you do all this?"

I shrugged, embarrassed. Some need of mine, exposed like this. "He was alone," I said. "Where are you going to go now?"

"Far, far," she said. "Now that we have our son, we can make the arrangements."

Félix and his father were standing shoulder to shoulder at the railing, and his father was speaking to him, but I couldn't catch the words.

"He has a cat in Peekskill," I said.

"A cat?"

"I'm sure he'll tell you," I said. "But you may be taking a cat to wherever you're going."

She looked puzzled and then laughed. "We'll take a dozen cats," she said. "Whatever he wants."

CHAPTER 22

I thought of getting back onto the West Side Elevated Highway, but instead I drove south through Washington Heights and Harlem, down into the Upper West Side. I was passing the enormous building site for the new concert hall on Columbus Avenue when I realized I was only a few blocks from where she lived.

I had only a minute to decide what I wanted to do. I turned onto West Sixty-Second Street, thinking that if I didn't see a place to park, I would just go on home — that was the kind of game I played all the time. It was not a fortuitous place for parking, but I saw a space almost immediately, not fifty yards from Central Park. I backed in, turned off the engine, and climbed out right away, hoping I would be at her door before I lost my nerve.

I was on fire with a willingness to humiliate myself. I walked north, glancing up now and then at the warmly lit facades of the grand apartment buildings whose upper windows looked out over the trees in the park. Something had shifted. Not long ago I wouldn't have dreamed of doing something this stupid, but now the alternative, which was to go home again and leave everything unsaid for another day, to find my things just where I had left them and wake to another late morning in the quiet house, my dignity intact and my life utterly unchanged, felt false and useless. There was a thinness to this kind of self-preservation. It required so much evasion and restraint, and there was no reward in the end, not really. There was no proctor watching this test, to congratulate me on having avoided once again the possibility of looking foolish or dependent, hurt or unprepared. There was no prize waiting for the person who needed the least.

I turned onto Sixty-Third Street, pursued by the wind, and passed the immense hulk of the YMCA, like a ship at anchor with lights lost in its upper reaches. The boardinghouse where Max had told me she lived huddled in its shadow, trying to match it with gothic touches around the windows and gutters. It was called, as she had said, the Aurora. The words were set in the concrete above the door, somewhat diminished by a more cheerful and modern sign that hung just below it, which said ROOMS TO LET FOR YOUNG WOMEN. I pushed through into a small lobby tiled in blue, like a changing room at a public pool. A watchman who looked as if sunlight never touched his face was sitting at the front desk, turning the pages of a newspaper.

"I'm here to see Maxine Comstock," I said.

He moved slowly to a black telephone on the desk and dialed a few numbers. "A visitor here for you," he said. I sat on a bench along the wall to wait, my heart clanging in my chest.

She came down after a few minutes, the slip of her, turning at the foot of the stairs. She was dressed in pink. I stood up, then didn't know what to do.

"Vera!" she said, for all the world as if she were happy to see me. She came and kissed my cheek. I tried to find my voice. "Are we going out?" she said. "I can get my coat."

"Yes, out," I croaked.

She went upstairs and I tried to compose myself. Some girls came in, bustling through the lobby, unlocking their mailboxes with tiny keys. Then Max was back, with her coat and handbag.

"Well," I said, uncertain, because I had planned only as far as a statement of grievances. "Let's go."

Out on the sidewalk I could feel her peering at me. I didn't know what to do with my face. My brain was filled with Lois's voice saying *Key West.* Not having anywhere in mind to go, and not wanting to ask her for suggestions, I led us to Central Park West, to the low stone wall along the edge of the park and the desolate benches. Men in suits streamed uptown.

"Are you all right?" Max said. She hadn't put on a hat, and her pale hair lifted and tangled around her face. We stood under a fringe of bare trees that leaned over the wall. There were stragglers in the park, people who had been caught by the early twilight and were now making their way to the exits, lit by the tall poles along the paths.

I saw now the problem with my course of action. Before, I had always relied on others to open the arguments that I planned to win. Here I had come to her, and therefore would have to begin this confrontation myself, which was a weak way to advance the weak position that she had hurt me and I was sad.

"I looked for you a month ago," I said, taking a deep breath. "Lois told me you had gone to Key West with another girl."

Her mouth opened. She leaned closer, then leaned back. "Sure, I did. I got back ages ago. I thought I might see you around — I tried you once or twice, but you were never home."

"If you had another girl," I said, staring intently into the park as if there were anything at all worth looking at in there, "you could have just said so."

"Another girl? Who, Sandra?" She laughed. "Wait, Vera, did you think I had thrown you over?" I was still facing away and she took hold of the lapel of my coat. "You're mad at me," she said, surprised.

"Well, I thought maybe," I said, but the rest of the sentence escaped me. Maybe we had started something. Maybe I was on your mind, more than the rest.

"Sandra was my roommate at Vassar," she said. "She's getting a divorce, so we went to Florida and lay around drinking piña coladas for a week. She's straight as a hatpin, Vera."

I was taken aback. "But Lois —"

"Lois is the worst gossip. Lois likes to imagine everyone else is having more fun than she is."

I tried to find my footing. She was still holding on to my coat.

"I just was never sure if you — if you felt like I did," I said. "The way you stayed in Poughkeepsie that day — and it was always hard to reach you. It just seemed like maybe I was making a fool of myself. So I stopped."

"You're such a coward," she said. In a smooth gesture she worked her hand in between the buttons of my coat, and I felt her thumb press against my stomach. I started and nearly fell on her. She was a shade shorter than I was and she looked up at me laughing, her other hand winding around the back of my neck, into my hair. "God forbid you be a fool," she said.

There were people everywhere, but no one looked at us. It was the woods so close by, the new darkness, the smell of thaw, two days now past the equinox. No one could intrude. A simple idea began to knit itself together between us. She put both hands in my pockets. "Come up," she said.

ACKNOWLEDGMENTS

This book would not be here without:

Masie Cochran, as brilliant as she is kind, and Soumeya Bendimerad Roberts, who has been both an advocate and a friend; Craig Popelars, a force, and the focus and intelligence of Elizabeth DeMeo and Alyssa Ogi on the editorial team; Jakob Vala, who has the eye and the range, and Diane Chonette, who brings it all together; the tireless efforts of the most pleasant people on earth, Nanci McCloskey, Molly Templeton, and Yashwina Canter; my writing group and first readers, always, Bonnie Altucher, Tom Cook, Helen Terndrup, and Jenna Leigh Evans; my parents, Peter and Katie Knecht, and brother, Rastus Knecht, who have helped and encouraged us through the most difficult two years that we've ever had or hope to have again; my mother-in-law, Elsa T. Leonida, who watched our baby and cooked us dozens of meals while I finished final edits on this book in an upstairs room; and Mark, who survived and keeps surviving, and whose first impulse is always to be generous.

This book is here in spite of:

Grief, love, and bed bugs. Pregnancy, social work, Brooklyn, the Q train, Pioneer Supermarket, laundry, a wrist brace, the blue screen of death, the stairs at 14th Street, moving twice, Twitter, a gas leak, whoever kept hacking my credit card, political despair, not enough fun and not enough sleep, occasionally too much fun, all my friends who left town, the worst thing that ever happened to us, and the best thing that ever happened to us.

READER'S GUIDE

1. When Vera first opens her detective agency, she finds that a number of clients are reluctant to work with her because she's a woman. What kinds of barriers to entry did you perceive for women in her industry? Do you think any of those barriers still exist today?

2. At the start of this book, Vera has recently finished decorating her home. What do you think Vera's house symbolizes to her?

3. New York City during the 1960s is a character in its own right. In what ways are the city and time period significant — thematically and atmospherically — as backdrops to Vera's story?

4. How does Vera's recent breakup influence her actions?

5. When Vera rents her office space, the landlord suggests that the front room could be where her "girl" would sit. Vera replies that she "would have to be my own girl." What do you think Vera means when she says this?

6. When were you most afraid for Vera's safety?

7. As Vera hunts down the secrets of others, she keeps her own close. What do you think is her single biggest secret, and who is she hiding it from?

8. How do you think Vera and Maxine's relationship would be different if it occurred in the present day? How has the landscape in America changed for queer women since the 1960s?

9. Why do you think there are so few adult novels starring female detectives?

10. What do you think the future holds for Vera Kelly?

ABOUT THE AUTHOR

Rosalie Knecht is the author of *Who Is Vera Kelly?* and *Relief Map*. She is the translator of César Aira's *The Seamstress and the Wind* (New Directions) and a Center for Fiction Emerging Writer Fellow. She lives in New Jersey.